Thomas Northway = Polly Burke
(1632–1702)
b. Burnet, England
d. Freetown, Mass.
...an of Rhode Island, 1664

Fortunatus Northway = Elizabeth Elting
(1798–1838)   (1805–1866)
b. Livingston Manor, N.Y.   b. Oyster Bay, N.Y.
d. Hudson, N.Y.   d. Hudson, N.Y.

...a Northway = Clarissa Hunter   Edward Ovid Northway = Alvinia Percepta Pierce
"Lige"   (1856–1894)   (1847–1936)   (1845–1940)
...37–1898)   b. Oxford, England   b. Whiskeyville, N.Y. b. Bloomfield, Ohio
...skeyville, N.Y. d. Ashtabula, Ohio   d. Bloomfield, Ohio   d. Ashtabula, Ohio
...tabula, Ohio

...a Burke Bailey   Thomas Northway = Matilda Elton   Harry Emerson Northway = Janet Pringle
(1866–1948)   "Tom Northway"   "Mattie"   (1898–1965)   (1917–1977)
...ific Junction, Calif. (1876–1966)   (1882–1946)   b. Bloomfield, Ohio   b. Toledo, Ohio
...reenwich, Conn.   b. Bloomfield, Ohio b. Ashtabula, Ohio d. Ashtabula, Ohio   d. Ashtabula, Ohio
                     d. Mesopotamia, Ohio d. Cleveland, Ohio

...cus Northway "Mark" = Louise Hathaway Whitlock   Lellie Northway = Morris Lanier
(1903–1968)   (1906–1985)   (1908–1972)   (1907–1969)
b. Cleveland, Ohio   b. Wabash, Ind.   b. Cleveland, Ohio b. Philadelphia, Penn.
d. Dallas, Tex.   d. Dallas, Tex.   d. Beach Haven, Fla. d. Beach Haven, Fla.

...e Whitlock Northway   Joy Louise Northway
(1933–)   (1936–)
b. Cleveland, Ohio   b. Akron, Ohio

MY FATHER'S HANDS

The Northway Series
TOM NORTHWAY
MY FATHER'S HANDS
NEW CREATIONS
A DEATH IN LOUISIANA

MY FATHER'S HANDS

PERSEVERANT·DABITUR

Marshall Terry

TEXAS TECH UNIVERSITY PRESS

This book was set in 11 on 15 ITC Garamond and printed on acid-free paper that
meets the guidelines for permanence and durability of the Committee on
Production Guidelines for Book Longevity of the Council on Library Resources. ⊗

Cover art by Paul Milosevich.
Jacket and book design by Kelley Ferguson Farwell.

Manufactured in the United States of America

Library of Congress Cataloging-in-Publication Data
Terry, Marshall, 1931-
   My Father's Hands / Marshall Terry.
       p.   cm. — (Northway series)
   ISBN 0-89672-274-0
   I. Title. II. Series: Terry, Marshall, 1931- Northway series.
PS3570.E699M9 1992
813'.54—dc20   91-16429
                                                    CIP

Texas Tech University Press
Lubbock, Texas 79409-1037 USA

92 93 94 95 96 97 98 99 / 9 8 7 6 5 4 3 2 1

To my brother and my sister,
and with gratitude to Bro Halff

I began in Ohio.
I still dream of home.
　　　James Wright
　　　"Stages On A Journey Westward"

Yet why not say what happened?
Pray for the grace of accuracy
Vermeer gave to the sun's illumination
stealing like the tide across a map
to his girl solid with yearning.
We are poor passing facts,
warned by that to give
each figure in the photograph
his living name.
　　　　　　Robert Lowell
　　　　　　"Epilogue"

It was only an old beer bottle floating across the foam.
It was only an old beer bottle far away from home.
Inside was a piece of paper with these words written on:
Whoever finds this bottle will find that the beer's all gone . . .
　　　　　　　　College song '24

THE INHERITANCE

My father's hands woke me by roughly shaking me that morning, those usually firm but gentle hands shaking me in anger.

"Yes, sir?" I said, feeling terrible, dopey, a little sick.

I was 17, just finished my junior year at my little school on the Hill. I had been out late with my girlfriend Ruth, had drunk sweet blackberry wine with my friend Wolf before being with Ruth, had come home deep into the night and sat on our front porch and finished the wine, then fallen asleep on the old glider there. Now I saw the sun was up. It was a marvelous early summer morning.

"Your mother has been worried sick," my father said, the frames of the glasses over his deep brown eyes glinting, his handsome face stern. "Don't you ever do that to her again."

"What?" I said.

My mother had waked in the early morning hours and not found me in my room. She had not thought to look out on the porch. She had not waked my father either, but kept her vigil until dawn, then until he awoke. She was like that: he must have his sleep; somehow I must be all right.

I stumbled up, roughly shaken awake, and went past my father and his anger in to her.

"I'm sorry," I said, hugging her, my slim, lovely mother. "I fell asleep, out there—"

She was in her robe. She had composed her face.

"It's all right," she said. "I was worried. You've never before—Come on, I'm making breakfast."

My brother and sister were at the kitchen table. Luke was fifteen, Joy twelve. They looked at me, and at our mother and father, wondering how to play it. I thought I saw a glint of relish behind Luke's thick lenses at it being his perfect older brother, for once, in the doghouse. They were eating eggs and bacon. The plate of my father's finished breakfast sat by them.

"Hey," I said. "I apologize to everyone."

"I bet you were out with Ruth," Joy said.

Feeling queasy, I sat down at the table with them. Mom put a glass of milk in front of me. Usually I would drink a quart a day.

"You don't look like you feel too well," my father said. He was ready to turn the Chrysler around in the driveway and go to work. He always left for work at 7:30. "You look a little blue around the gills. Couldn't have anything to do with that wine bottle you had cradled in your arms, could it?"

At that I looked and saw the yellow egg streaks and the hardened bacon fat left on his plate, and rose, with the pressure in my throat, and made a sort of bow to the glistening white kitchen wall and with a mighty rush, as of the Hoover dam, decorated the wall with a striking splash of purple.

My sister Joy screamed, half in fright, half in ecstasy.

Number One Son, the great Responsible, I stood there looking at the wall.

Then looked at my father.

The twinkle had come into his eye. He suddenly grinned.

"As the waiter inquired," he said, "will that be all, sir?"

He laughed. Then my brother Luke joined in the laughing.

"Dago red?" Dad said. "I thought I told you about that stuff."

"No. Bla—" I was trying to utter Blackberry. "Never mind," I said.

My mother, no twinkle in her fine blue eyes, handed me a washrag, then set to work on the wall with a cloth.

"Aagh," said my bouncy little sister. "How do you expect us to eat?"

"I thought you were in training for football," said my father.

"I'm going into training today," I said, attempting a smile.

"Go get ready for work," he said. "You'll be late. It's okay. Good lesson for all you guys, about cheap wine. A little honest work, son, sweat it out, you'll be okay."

"Wolf and I—" I said.

"It's okay," he said. "Now remember what I told you bums to do around here today. Luke?"

My round-bodied, long-legged, burr-headed brother hooded his eyes at our father. It was his famous cobra look.

I ate some cereal, took a sip of milk, and kissed my mother.

"Remarkable performance, old Bo," she said.

"How is Dad today?" I said.

"He is calmer," she said.

Then I was glad to start up my motor scooter and get out of there, to escape the assigned tasks our father always had for us around the place, to retreat from the tasks of children to "man's work," to rip along on the old red scooter down the treelined winding roads to Park Village.

The year was 1948. It was still a time of innocence for those of us growing up on our wooded hill a dozen miles beyond the limits of our Ohio river city. The "fallout" of the war had not yet rained down change and corruption upon the order and values of my place and family.

My father, Marcus Northway, was of farmer stock and dearly loved those seven acres of land he had brought us up out of the city to a few years before. Loved, as we all did, our Shawnee Run road and all the roads that once were Indian paths and the woods all around us, once the roaming grounds of the Shawnee and the Iroquois. Loved our plain old comfortable house, our long sweep of grassy yard in

4

front, our side apple orchard and back fields for corn and potatoes and grapes and berries, all the growing things that my father, like his father, cherished. And the woods of maple, ash, elm, oak, and blacklocust trees beyond.

My father was early forties then, my mother younger, and we were a happy family there. Indeed the family myth said that it was Paradise, the Garden to be tended.

I was late in pulling up to the town maintenance building down in Park Village, but it didn't seem to matter. Our truck sat there hunched upon its big wheels. My buddy Wolf was laid out on the driveway in his work duds catching winks. Baldy was leaning against the cab smoking. Vince was drinking coffee from a thermos. He was a short man whose age would have been hard to guess. He wore a necktie to drive the garbage truck. Baldy was a long lean man so seamed he appeared to be old, but he must have been younger than my father.

"Have a late night, did you?" Vince said.

Wolf rolled over, looking at me.

Smoking, Baldy said, "Old Bo had him a late night last night, I'd say."

Vince looked up at the bright blue summer sky. They said he had been mayor of this village here, but now he had a "problem."

"Going to be a hot one," he declared.

"Going to be a hot one today," said Baldy. "Well, sir, if Prince Charming here has got his jock on straight and is ready, maybe we can get this here show on the road."

5

Vince and Baldy got up in the cab. Wolf and I took our places hanging off the back of the truck, wearing heavy canvas gloves.

"I don't know if I can do this today," I said. "I got sick on that stupid wine."

"Tough it out," Wolf said, flexing his biceps. "You'll never have a better deal, Bo. Seventy-five cents an hour and all you can eat—"

"Thanks, buddy."

Riding the truck, after we had sharked up and emptied into the bin the first cans in the alley and I found I wasn't going to be sick, I began thinking about Ruth, of holding her the night before. We'd slipped into old lady Marlow's pool and after we'd swum in our underwear I'd held her tightly for a moment at the pool's edge. Our love was "pure," and our frustration growing, so early in the summer. I had gone home with "passion pains" and drunk the damnable sweet blackberry wine before blotting out upon the glider. Going down the alley on the garbage truck I began to think of how strange and hard it was, the way the world was set up, for young people who were supposed to be too young to get involved, and really weren't.

"What are you thinking?" Wolf said, as we jammed cans back in their alley holders. "You ain't said boo."

"I was thinking I was going to stay home tonight, and write."

I was trying to write some stories, thinking they might become a novel. They were verbose and romantic, under the influence of *Look Homeward, Angel*, read continually on

6

the porch in that old glider through the late spring, with the buds coming out on the apple trees within my sight.

"Great," Wolf said. He read only *Popular Mechanics*, but was proud of the ambition of his buddy. "I liked that story you did last year about the ziggy fighter."

"Mr. Ash didn't. He said there was too much corny dialect, that he was a cliche of a Negro. He said I shouldn't write about things I didn't know."

"I liked it when old Adonis Jackson beat the hell out of that guy that had beaten up his brother."

"I took that from another story."

"So what? How many plots are there? So what are you writing now?"

I was trying to write about visiting my grandfather Luke and Remember, my grandmother, and falling in love with my beautiful cousin, a gorgeous creature my own age, there in the mountains of California, the summer before; but I did not want to tell Wolf that.

"I'll write about you," I said.

"All right," he said. "You do that, Bo. Write about how Rebecca's father told her not to see me anymore. Jesus, you know I wouldn't do nothing with Rebecca, Bo. I'm going to Ault Park tonight. Dime a dance, listen to the music, find me another dolly. Maybe just get in a fight. You write a story about the great lover who lost the one girl he ever really loved—God, look how this slob keeps his cans! Maybe we should buy him some lids —"

That afternoon we took a lighter truck and a couple of two-handled saws and went to work cutting up two giant

7

trees, then digging out the stumps, in a recreational park there in the village.

Vince, problem or not, worked steadily and well at his end of the saw across from Wolf. Baldy was my partner. He was tireless, but I was also good at this, for my father had taught me the use of saw and ax and spade at the many tasks on our place.

"I don't know why the Village wants these trees down," Vince said. He was in coveralls now, seemingly the most measured and meticulous of men. "I would have voted against it. There aren't so many trees this old. Big old trees like these are worth leaving live."

"There are about four hundred trees in this here park," Baldy said. "They wanted some light to get through to them swings there so's the kids could see to use 'em."

"Ridiculous," said Vince, doing the work he did not approve of.

Vince and Wolf talked as they worked. Baldy rarely spoke while working.

I thought of my father's hands shaking me awake this morning. I thought of how patiently he had taught me the use of this crosscut saw. "Up and down, son," he'd say. "That's right. Easy does it. Don't let it bind, or spring back at you. Give it its path, son. Okay, now you're doing it. Let the saw do the work."

I thought of my father's hands, their strength and steadiness.

His hands had strong, blunt fingers with well-kept nails whose moons were white like shell. The tufts of hair beneath the knuckles were soft, almost feminine. They were the hands of a salesman, an entrepreneur who loved the romance of American business (how much an anomaly this was, the farmer's stern Puritan ethic blended with the ad man's enthusiastic consumerism, I did not realize until much later in my life) but from continuous outdoor work the calluses were firmly like the rind to the melon one with them. He had a grip strong as the vise on the work table in our tool shed, as his father, the true farmer up north of us in our Ohio, now seventy, also had. My father wore an earthen-toned ring of soft grayblue-orangy-agaty colors on a finger of his right hand.

Those hands had never struck me, or my brother or my sister. That morning's shaking was the roughest treatment I had gotten, and it came because of my mother's worry.

Now, sweating hard, working across from long lean Baldy, I thought of moments upon moments of my father's hands, doing the yeoman tasks around the place, forever teaching us how to sweep, to use a broom, to do the simplest job right, this way, son, see, so the broom doesn't go back over where you've already swept; or, on my shoulders, as I was trying to learn the box step so I could shine in Madame Federova's dance class: one, two, three; one, two, three, four, marching me up and down to music, trying to teach me, like a drill sergeant, rhythm, dance. Hoeing the spuds. Catching the frog or cricket, putting it on the hook, throwing the line on the bamboo pole out into the lake just so; pulling in the fish, taking out the hook, one hand here, the other there . . .

"Good work, Bo," said Baldy, as we took a last long clean swipe and the chunks dropped neatly down between us.

At four o'clock, aching, sweated out in the hot summer afternoon but happy being dark from sun and hardening in muscle, I had the absolute feeling within me that I would be young forever. We laid off and stopped for a beer at the Village Tavern, a cool dark place where they would serve me and Wolf on Vince's and Baldy's say-so.

"Good day," Vince said, draining down his Red Top ale.

"Good day out there today," Baldy said. "We got it done out there today."

That evening my father came home looking tired. Coming in the door he looked incongruous, or comic, to me, wearing a brown double-breasted suit that seemed too heavy for the season, and his yellow bow tie, and with his old brown Dobbs hat upon his head. He stopped to sniff at the aroma of the roast my mother was cooking. She was fixing a dinner that would have fitted Sunday or a holiday more than midweek. Something was up.

I sat reading, curled in a chair in a corner of the living room, as my father came in the room with a letter Mom had handed him. She followed him into the room as he stood on the red-and-blue patterned Turkish rug and read the letter.

"What does Harry say, Mark?" my mother asked.

He shook his head. I thought I saw a slight trembling in the hand that held the letter.

"He won't do it. He and Janet don't see any reason to contest it."

My great-spirited father's face in that moment looked mean, rigid. Not lively mad but as if he were wearing some sort of mask.

"Why dear," she said, in her gentle, placating voice that at times like that when its tone was so opposite to his mood must have driven him up the wall, "you didn't really think they would, did you? Why don't you go up and lie down for a while before dinner, Mark? You mustn't let it upset you. I think I can understand why they wouldn't—"

"Sure! You can always seem to understand the other guy's position! How about mine, ours? By God, Louise—"

"Mark! Oh, Bo's here—"

I was sitting there damned if I'd retreat, wanting to hear it, the Hardy novel in my lap growing pale and remote. I had seldom heard raised voices or harsh tones between my parents.

Vaguely I knew what the matter was. Our great-aunt Ida, widow of old General Marcus Northway, the millionaire, who had kicked off years before, had now died herself. Aunt Ida, I knew, had lived somewhere up in Connecticut, some cold, bleak place I could not imagine. The General's wealth and Aunt Ida's tyranny and aggrandizement of the family name had been the chief lore of our family as we kids were growing up.

"Well," Dad said, with a look in my direction. "Of course not, Lou. I would not want to get upset. Why, it's no big deal, is it? Just getting euchred out of twenty, thirty million dollars that by all rights should be ours—!"

11

"We're not even sure of the amount until we see the whole will, Mark. It must have taken so much of it to care for her all these years—"

"Of course Harry won't fight it!" my father exploded. "Harry never thought he'd get a penny—Oh, that was clever, giving us all a little payoff, spreading out some chickenfeed to keep the chickens happy— I'll tell you about this, son. So now I guess I am just supposed to sit back and take a royal rooking from two of the biggest crooks since Jesse James!"

He wadded up the letter, his hand shaking now, and threw it on the rug that had been given to them by Aunt Ida and Uncle Marcus after one of their trips to Asia.

"I knew I should have gone to see her! 'Oh no,' the damn nurse said, 'it's better not to disturb her now'—"

"Mark. Dear. Please."

He stood, a big man, taller than I would ever be, flushed, the glasses on his Roman nose a little crooked, looking out the window at the twilight summer beauty of the red-appled trees in the orchard, and beyond, within himself, to a hope or dream he'd had.

My mother stooped to pick up the wadded letter. Straightening she grimaced, the damnable arthritis in her back twinging. She looked at me, shaking her head slightly. Dad turned from staring out the window, and they looked at each other.

"What's for dinner?" he said.

She smiled. My mother's hair was more light brown than the blond it had been; her eyes were a blue of sometimes calm, sometimes sternly deep water, a color that blazed in her mother's eyes but took on more muted tones in hers; she was fairly tall, but delicate in form and feature.

"Pot roast. And I've made an apple grunt, just especially for my guy."

"I'll bet you made that apple grunt," he said, suddenly grinning and winking at me. "Sounds good, don't it, Bo? I'll tell you all about this, son. You deserve to know about it. Maybe we should have a family conference. Now I think I will go upstairs, rest up for that apple grunt. It's been a day. That damn Hoppy—"

I followed my mother into the wonderful-smelling kitchen whose wall I had decorated that morning.

"Did you see his hand shaking?" I said.

For a moment her eyes blazed. "You must not mention that," she said. "I'm trying to get him to go to a doctor and see about it. But don't you let him know you notice it, now. He'll hardly talk to me about it. It's obviously his nerves, because of this terrible—this will of that terrible old woman. She always tried to dominate our—your father's—life, and now finally, thank God, she's dead . . ."

I waited a minute to say anything, smelling the aromas of pot roast and the cobbler. Then I said, "He didn't get any dough? In Aunt Ida's will?"

"Shh. He'll want to tell you himself. Yes, we got some, that 'chickenfeed' he spoke of. A few token thousands—just exactly what everyone else got. What Uncle Harry and Janet got, and your Aunt Lellie, even Gramp. Oh, he's right—it was clever! Gramp Tom laughed. He hated the way General Marcus had dictated to him in his own life, and how old Marcus and Ida tried to take over

13

your father's life, and he never got along with Ida. Gramp Tom thought his getting anything at all from them was a huge joke. But it infuriated your father, the injustice of it. Because—well, it's a long story, surely not a kitchen story, Bo. I'm not even sure how much you know. I better finish getting dinner now."

"Because he was supposed to be like their own son—be 'Marcus Northway the Second'?"

"Yes."

"And they took him out of Ohio State where he was happy playing tennis and the ukulele and made him go to Yale and start all over again as a freshman?"

"How did you know that?"

"From Gramp. And I've gone through the albums and seen Dad and General Marcus in the pictures, like them visiting him at Yale in that Rolls Royce with a chauffeur. And he changed his middle name so his name would be the same as the General's—"

"And later changed it back again so it wouldn't be."

"And then they even wanted me to be 'Marcus Northway Third' and sent all that silver to me when I was a baby with those initials engraved on it—"

"In the very depth of the Depression, when we literally did not have enough to—" Mom made a face, lifting the roast from the oven. "Well. That is enough of that, for now. Okay? Go round up the others, tell them it's ready, will you, Marcus Third?"

"So who got it all?"

"What all?"

"The twenty, thirty million."

14

"Oh pooh. I think it's hardly that. She lived so long, poor old Ida, she got so sick and half-crazy after Uncle Marcus died, she had to have so much care. But there's the rub, that's what your father cannot stand, what so offends his sense of justice. Because, you see, Bo, Miss McAdoo, the *nurse*, Aunt Ida's loyal nurse for fifteen years, Miss McAdoo and Aunt Ida's *lawyer*, why, *they* got it! Those two together obviously in collusion got it all: whatever fortune there was left, and the three houses, in Greenwich, Connecticut there and in Florida and in California, and all the *stuff*. I mean, what incredible things they had, from all over the world, so many things like the lamp and rug we have!"

"Damn!" I said. "That would burn your butt! The lawyer and the nurse! Not even family at all!"

My mother pretended to frown. "I will burn your whatever, if you don't stop such language. Now go tell the others."

I reached to pick off a hot end piece of the roast. "Hell," I said, bigshot, smacking my lips, "what would we do with all that dough? Who needs it?"

"That's what I say," she said.

At the dinner table he seemed himself again. Yet he sat holding the serving spoon and fork as Joy went on and on with the blessing, mentioning all the poor people who had nothing to eat, the starving Chinese and Armenians, and all the dogs and cats in the world. When Joy finished he said to her abruptly from the head of the table, "You don't have to pray forever for it to be heard, you know."

Joy's china-blue eyes and round pink face fell as if he had hit her. She lived, this loving girl, to please him.

"Mark!" my mother said, even more sharply than she had in the living room before.

He got up and walked around the table and leaned to kiss Joy.

"That's all right, baby," he said. "Daddy is tired tonight. That was a fine prayer. You pray as long as you want to, sweetheart."

"I thought it was pretty long myself," Luke said. He sat watching the roast like a hawk eyes its prey.

After dinner Dad went in the living room with its Turkey rug from Aunt Ida and the General and sat in his favorite chair by the rose and green vine and flower-patterned lamp that the old couple had acquired in China in the twenties and held the new Satevepost in his lap. There was a serial by James Warner Bellah in it that he was looking forward to reading. He liked good "yarns" read in the *Post* or *Bluebook* and thought maybe that was what I was after in my professed interest in "writing." He thought that was okay, but did not hide from me that he considered fiction a trivial form. He considered that the writing that was worthwhile now was informative instruction about what was really happening in our Red-menaced world.

That night he and my mother went upstairs together early.

Later, when I went up, going by their door I saw that they were in their robes sitting up in bed side by side with my mother reading aloud from *The Sermon on the Mount,* their favorite book by the spiritualist Emmet Fox. Now I see that they were in that Platonic-Augustinian-Emersonian line of spiritual belief that equates evil with ignorance. And now it's clear to me that such a concept cannot really soothe one's righteous anger when evil does appear. She was reading to him a passage concerning the Spiritual Key.

Joy was sleeping soundly, dreaming of starving Chinese and her father angry with them. I went down to the end of the hall to my brother's room, but at his closed door smelled the smoke from his secret cigaret and retreated back up the hallway, stopping at the small "den" room which, in its array of photos and mementos, held the nonspiritual key to my father's problem, to his disappointment and his anger.

My father had set up this room as a memorial to the person his name came from, a reminder to us that we'd had one "Great Man" in the family. I stepped inside and switched on the light.

On one wall I saw photos of Uncle Marcus with notables: arm in arm with Luther Burbank at the place in California where Burbank experimented with flowers, vegetables, and trees, making his "new creations"; with Ford, and Firestone, and Rockefeller; with Edison standing in front of Edison's house surrounded by big-boled palm trees in Fort Myers, where the General had built a plush hotel where TR and other chums would come to fish the river or venture out for tarpon on the nearby deep. Next to these was a photo of Teddy himself, full length in bush jacket, leggings and boots, Western hat, and with machete, glowing with Manifest Destiny. This had been, after he married late, and married a Standard Oil widow, Uncle Marcus's world. Not to say he had not been a distinguished doctor first, and surgeon-general of his state and a surgeon in the rousing Spanish-American War.

I looked closely at his "official" portrait, central on the wall. Taken in his later years it showed the first Marcus Northway seated at a table set with crystal and silver in the suite he kept at the Waldorf-Astoria: fair, handsome, clear-eyed, with my father's Roman beak and firm mouth. Kind-looking, I thought, but with a don't-suffer-fools sternness, too.

Beside that was the large color photograph of Aunt Ida, a tank of a woman, not pretty certainly, all in lacy blue and a sun hat, and the General in a white suit standing under Japanese lanterns and Oriental-looking trees on the terrace of their gabled English lodge at Coronado.

I turned out the light in this museum, with its photos and old dress swords upon the walls, a room that had always held an air of musty fantasy for me, and went into my own familiar room.

I am not sure I have conveyed the depth of feeling I held for my father. If often absolute, he seemed always also kind, and a rock, so strong that now imagining his touch, the feel of worn flannel as I would jump into his arms as a boy, the rich timbre of his voice as he sang the family songs created by his father and himself, I can still recall that image of his strength. Stern, working us "like Trojans" around our place, he was also sentimental, and absolute in his caring and his committed love to us. And often humor would crackle out from around the rock like a lightning flash before or after storm. The times of his sudden relenting from his relentless pushing of himself and others, of letting go into lightheartedness, were times memorable for all of us, for my mother too.

That Saturday he rose early as usual and drove the Chrysler down off the Hill, through suburbs and along the expressway overlooking the river to his downtown office. When he returned at mid-morning I heard him complaining to Mom about Hoppy, his assistant at the station. My father had moved from his merchandising position with the big clear-channel radio station to be its first television station manager, thus accepting a great new challenge of the age. Since the heralded coaxial cable was not to arrive for a year or so, all the TV programming had to be devised and furnished locally. Dad often threatened, in desperation, to put on a minstrel show with us kids in blackface; to make Joy dance, Luke sing, me recite "The Raven." He was a steady reader of the Saint stories, by Leslie Charteris, and called his fat little hillbilly assistant "Hoppy" because the guy reminded him of the Saint's sidekick in the series, Hoppy Uniatz. I never knew what "Hoppy's" real name was, but I always felt he didn't much appreciate his nickname. Now he and Dad were in tension because the little prick wanted to cut some of the variety stuff and go real heavy with wrestling in the programming. My father disapproved of the wrestling. He explained to me how he had seen them bite down on sheep-blood pellets so the blood sprang from their mouths in the ring. He didn't like it because it was phony, crooked.

But this morning he seemed to be upset by the cap that Hoppy wore: an old cloth cap with a button on the top.

"I can smell the sweat in the band of that cap when he puts it on. It smells like the Depression. It makes me feel sick. For fifteen bucks the damn fool could buy himself a hat!"

He changed into his baggy khakis and flannel shirt and floppy farmer's hat and came outside, smoking a rare Spud, to review his troops.

Finding that Luke had not made it out of his room yet, he yelled for him. Luke had been instructed to mow the side meadow. I was up on a ladder painting the old barn, a summer ritual. We painted it up to the very top where the ladder would not reach. Up there it remained an old cracked brown.

Dad rolled the two-wheeled Gravely tractor out of the barn as Luke came outside. With a stone Dad sharpened the cutting blades and oiled and attached them. We all had our definitions, Dad's working catalogue of what we each did best. Luke was the mechanical one; the Gravely, which he despised, was his baby. Now Luke stood watching Dad: just then all legs, with a short body, and the butch haircut he let grow so long it stood straight up on his round head like the field he didn't want to mow, and thick hornrim glasses. Dad got up from his squat and offered him the starter cord.

Luke did not move to take it.

"Denny and I thought we'd go down into town today," he said.

My father frowned.

"Well, I think you had better do your work first," he said. "You know Saturday is work day, son. If that field gets much higher we'll have to bale it. Just what did you and Denny think you were going to do?"

"Fool around."

Dad shook his head.

"Can we go later, this afternoon?"

"Where?"

"Oh, to the show. There's a show downtown, at the Orpheum."

"What, son?"

"It's a comedy." Luke squinted at him. "Some Chaplin films."

"I wouldn't fool with that," Mark Northway said.

"You liked *The Great Dictator.*"

"Sure. He's a good actor, a good comedian. I'll grant you that. I just don't see why you would give your business and support to a Communist."

"Oh, Daddy! What difference does it make, in a movie, if he is—"

"You better not plan to go today, Luke. We have enough to do here to hold us, today."

"Damn!" Luke said.

Our father did not give him the satisfaction of thinking that he heard it.

"Well, can we go tomorrow?"

"I thought we might all go to the ball game tomorrow, you and me and Bo and Joy. Blackwell's going to pitch."

Luke made a face. He could not stand baseball. Strange to our father, Luke liked, even then, weird things like opera and ballet.

21

"You don't have to go," the big guy said. He stood, shaking his head, as Luke started off, the machine pulling him into the field. Then he watched me for a while, to be sure I was not slopping the paint and not in position to fall off the ladder, then moved to the plowed field of corn and all the other stuff to be sure that Joy was getting her buckets of water to the roots and not on the leaves of the tomatoes.

Later, stiff, I climbed down off the ladder and stretched, then headed into our back woods where my father had built a tree house in a stout tall oak tree for us right after we had moved out here to the Hill from down in the city. Ruth was on my mind, and our relationship, and my parents' admonition that we were getting too serious, too bound up together too young. While I didn't much yet care one way or the other, I knew that my father wanted me to go on to college as a stepping stone to some great career, as the old General had wished for him.

Standing by that tree, which later I came to remember and think of shamelessly as the Bo Tree, I thought of sitting scrunched up close to Ruth on its little platform half way up a year ago. (I had been "going steady," more or less, with Ruth for more than two years by now.) First I was telling her stories. She would let me kiss her after the ones she liked. I told her of when, for my mother's health, her recovery from arthritis, we had lived for half a year without our father but with my grandmother Remember on an island with a magic name: Sanibel. I told her the water was salt and the sun hot and when our father came to visit we led him into the stickerburrs on the sand and he yelled and jumped around and made us laugh. Shells of all whorls and

22

colors on the beach, swept by currents of both the Gulf and the great ocean. A whale swept up on the beach, a huge dead whale lying there stinking among the shells on the beach. An old black lady tall as a tree who wore a turban and cooked for us turtle meat that squirmed in the skillet on the stove. How Bo walked with her, Katie, along beside salt marshes in the island's interior on a dark sandy path where an alligator a mile long came out at us, the woman and the boy of five. "Shoo! Go 'way! Look out!" Katie said, and the gator did as he was told.

Ruth kissed me and said, "I think you'll be a writer, if that's what you want, Bo. I bet you'll be good. It makes me feel happy, but sad too. Mother barely even knows you, but she's warning me already. She says it'll be okay for now, but then I'll get hooked on you and then—Then you'll go off, to college and—My Daddy is about half crazy, he always was wanting to be a writer—"

Then she held me very tight, and we held on to each other for a moment, too young of course to know or imagine what life and time would bring. "Don't worry," I'd said then. "We have forever 'til I even have to think about it, college and all that. I really don't think Hemingway or Faulkner or Thomas Wolfe or any of them even went to college. Have you ever heard of a writer that didn't just go out in the world, like around the world on a tramp steamer, having adventures and getting experiences to write about—of a writer who wasted time in college?"

"How would I know?" Ruth said. "We had to read *Great Expectations* this year in class, and old Charles Dickens had

23

to really suffer and work in something horrible sounding called a blacking factory."

"In that case I'll go to college," I said, trying to kiss her again, but she pushed away. But I grabbed her—we almost fell fifteen feet to the tangle of poison ivy and brush below—and said, "Plenty of room on a tramp steamer for two, I bet." I got another kiss for that.

Now, I touched the rough bark of the tree, and turned back out of the woods and walked over the plowed and planted ground to the paved ground and the barn and the ladder and climbed back up with my brush and paint bucket and got to work.

The next day our father felt so mellow after Sunday roast that, astounding him, he let Luke go with his friend Denny to the Chaplin films. ("Just remember you are responsible for your choices in this life, son," he said to him.) Then he and Joy and I piled into the Chrysler and drove down to old Crosley Field to see the Reds play the Pirates and our hero Ewell "The Whip" Blackwell pitch. Dad seemed thoroughly happy, whistling "Take Me Out to the Ball Game" on the way.

It was a good game. Already I was taking baseball as a metaphor and keeping its images in my mind for doing well or poorly at something. I loved its sense of readiness, its sense that you must come through with individual effort when it counted.

"The Whip" was brilliant, coiling around the batters sidearm so the Pirates hardly saw the ball until it was in Lamanno's mitt. Their little Rojek bunted and caught Grady Hatton, the Reds' cocky third baseman, off guard, and a couple of guys got hold of it to right, but Blackwell was never in trouble. Wyrostek of the Reds, moving like a wand out in center, made a catch against the wall to help him out. Then Hank Sauer parked one over the left-field fence into "Burgerville." Bobby Adams, the second sacker, cracked a homer too, a line drive that just kept rising and cleared the fence by a few inches at the flag. The game went 4-1 to the Reds, Bucky Walters coming on to relieve Blackwell in the eighth.

When we got home Luke was laid out on the purple and deep-blue rug in the living room with the funnies, peering through Terry, Annie and Punjab and the Asp, the Little King, Blondie and Prince Valiant. We all settled down to read in there. Just before seven Mom brought in the toasted roast-beef sandwiches and cocoa and we turned on the radio to hear an hour of Jack Benny and Edgar Bergen with Charlie McCarthy and Mortimer Snerd, a pretty smart rube in the American tradition, before I went to try to work on my young romantic story.

It was set where my brother Luke and I had visited up in the California mountains where my beloved other grandfather, Luke Whitlock, the judge, and my grandmother Remember had gone to make a new start. It was about first love. (As if, being still so young, you could write that!) My tiny grandmother, and my tall Grandfather Luke, picking up the 200-pound block of ice with tongs and swinging around and around with it so he could get momentum to carry it to the icehouse, in the mountains there; and the path through the woods to the small cold clear lake, and an arrow through my heart for my cousin: her teasing eyes, her brown legs in white short-shorts, her tawny hair just out of pigtails. Trying to be about all that.

Off in this reverie, I did not notice my mother at my doorway until I smelled the smoke from the Chesterfield she was lighting. I looked up, startled. She made a face, and shrugged.

"He says he is going up to Cleveland, next weekend," she said. "He's going to try to get Harry—and your Gramp—to help him fight it—"

Then he was at the doorway with her, and she had merged back into the hallway, merged with a wraith of smoke, like a genie.

"Ask Harry in person, son. Harry's a smart guy, he'll see it's right, when I talk to him. I thought you might go along with me, help drive. We'll take the little car. What do you say? Ruth will let you get away for one weekend, won't she?"

"Sure," I said. "I'll go."

The next Saturday we set off driving, in the Plymouth, in rain and darkness at 4:30 in the morning. My father believed in getting off early, like the truckers did, before the other guy was up. It was eight hours to Cleveland. He wanted to get to Uncle Harry's a little after noon, so we could go on to my grandfather's. My "Gramp"—my father's father, Tom Northway—had retired to an old farm that had been in the family for generations, in Geauga County, near Mesopotamia: the land between the rivers. Dad knew I loved it there with my Gramp, now playing his role of sage old farmer-clown to the enjoyment of all, and that I would rather spend the night there than at Harry's.

An hour into the trip a smudge of light pushed its way
up into the sky, like Mom's Dutch Cleanser scouring at the
rim of blackness of the world. Still, the sky seemed black as
iron. The rain beat down. Thinking I slept, my father said
nothing. He was driving carefully, his face total concentration, every so often his hand imperceptibly trembling on
the wheel. I remembered making this drive with Dad two
years before, when my grandmother Mattie died. It was
after that that Gramp had gone out to the farm from
Cleveland. That time too we set out in darkness, at night,
right after Gramp's call. Sleepy, my father had let me—only
15 then—drive. Now I remembered, with the same feeling
of my scrotum being squeezed, my father waking in the
passenger's seat as I, unknowing, unused to highway
driving, was heading full speed for one of those relic
one-way bridges on this road. "Slow down, son," he'd said.
"Now. Just slow her down and pull over on the shoulder."

Which I did, never questioning why because he was so
calm and then saw the headlights on the bridge, and the
other car come hurtling through.

Now we were going through Xenia. There was
something sinister about Xenia I could not quite place:
something about it being black.

I sat up and stretched, yawning, like an actor on the
stage.

"Hey there," he said.

"You said that you would tell me more about it."

"It's the principle of the thing, son," he said. "Hell, they
obviously rigged the deal. That Nurse McAdoo, and that
lawyer guy. Together, of course, they could do it—set her

27

up to sign another will. She was in her eighties, you know, and in none too good shape. I tried to go see her, up there, last year and the year before, but McAdoo told me it wouldn't be a good idea. Said each time that if I would just wait until Ida got a little better—I should have gone to see her. But who would ever have figured this—this highway robbery?"

He shook his head, then said: "We are the family, you know."

"You were always their favorite, weren't you?"

"Well, Bo, let's just say that over the years I paid my dues."

We pulled in to a Sohio station in the town of Delaware and both got out to use the rest room. It was raining just lightly now, the black of the sky breaking into puffy gray clouds. He said I could take the wheel for a while if I was awake.

At my first intersection I worked the clutch pedal and put the gear in neutral so I would not idle in third gear or ride the clutch. On green I concentrated on shifting cleanly through the gears. The Plymouth flowed ahead, the ship's emblem steady on the hood.

"That's the way, son," my father said.

When we hit the old red-brick stretch of road, near Lodi, he began to doze. Later he woke up all of a sudden, almost as if terrified, lurching forward to grab the dashboard, making me swerve the car.

"Be careful, son!" he cried.

Then he sat back. I kept driving carefully. Then he reached and put his hand on my shoulder.

"It's okay," he said. "Just watch the road. I had a dream. You're doing fine. It's okay. I just . . . woke up funny."

Harry lived in Shaker Heights. He and Aunt Janet lived now near the street where Tom and Mattie Northway had lived in Shaker Heights before, one night, she called out to him and died. I sat in a wicker rocker in Harry's glassed-in sun porch and thought how strange it was to be back here, remembering in detail that pretty red-brick, white-trimmed house and knowing it was still there, just blocks from where I sat, and that I would not be going into it or probably even see it. This house reminded me of it. Grandma Mattie had kept her yellow singing birds on their sun porch.

Now it had become a clear summer day. The sun flooded through the glass of the room. In the room beyond I could hear my father's and Uncle Harry's voices. They had been at it about an hour. I had retreated here. Now my father's voice began to rise.

He had brought a bunch of letters and papers in his briefcase and was showing them to Harry, his cousin who was a lawyer. Aunt Janet was sitting in there too, but she never peeped. She wore her hair in a bun. Uncle Harry was a handsome guy a little older than my father. They had been to the same college but not at the same time. They always had been friends. I remembered some jolly times, with Harry and Gramp and Dad, singing the old songs.

"This letter, Harry, for example, is signed both by Uncle Marcus and by Ida," my father's voice was saying. "It specifically says that they mean for me to have the Coronado house and that they will deed it to me later."

"But they did not do so, did they, Marcus?"

29

"No. Of course not. He died. But this letter stated their clear intention."

"Intentions won't suffice—"

"Intentions are everything, damn it! And later, many times, Ida said—"

"Marcus, Marcus! That letter is thirteen year old! All these notes and letters mean—well, nothing—now. Nor what he, or she, declared, from time to time . . . "

"What do you mean, they mean nothing? It was their constant intention. And everybody knew it, and you knew it—"

My father's voice sank low, the resonant timbre gone. It sounded weak and tired. I got up out of the warm circle of sunshine and walked into the cool, formal living room. As I did so Harry's voice said:

"You don't have a leg to stand on, Mark."

Coming in the room I looked at Dad, sitting incongruously in a velvety chair. It was the first time my father had ever looked small to me. His face seemed frozen in some strange expression, as of bewilderment, like a mask of my father's face. I started to go over to him; but knew I must not; so stood like a moron in the entrance to the room. Aunt Janet sat in the corner on a love seat like a doll with a broom up her back.

Then Dad grinned, his great old grin. The terrible moment passed. He sat up and looked his size, looked a lot bigger than his balding cousin Harry, and put the papers which were in his hands into the briefcase with his initials stamped on it in gold and said, with that grin on his mug like we were going fishing or about to attack a field of weeds with sharpened hoes or like he had just discovered Texas or some other fabulous section of the country, "Okay. I guess, Harry, whether they hold me up or not, my own are the only legs I'll have with me on this."

Harry looked at him, then nodded and turned to acknowledge me. "Well, young Mark, have you been catching a catnap out there? He's a fine boy, Marcus. I'll bet you have to fight the girls off, don't you, Bo? Your father says that you are interested in writing. Are you going to go to—" He mentioned the college they had both attended. "—like your old man did?"

"I don't know," I said. College was about the most remote concern in my mind just then.

"He won the 'Harvard Book' at his school. 'Knit one, purl two, Hahvahd woo woo,'" my populist father said.

"Well, that's fine. Just fine. I wouldn't overlook Harvard. I went to Law School there, you know."

"I know," Mark Northway said.

Aunt Janet asked if we did not want a snack before we left. She had not known exactly when to expect us, so had not counted on us for lunch, but she did have some little sandwiches and cupcakes.

"Have a beer," Harry said.

In the car Dad said, "Harry's okay. He's worked hard and done real well. He had said already he wouldn't go for it. I hoped he'd change his mind. He could at least testify, against those crooks, that it was well known—that the logical heir was not the nurse. But Harry and Janet got the same as your mother and I got from the will, and never expected to get a nickel."

31

He sat back, looking out the window as I drove; then began to whistle.

After we passed through the village of Mesopotamia and passed by houses with Amish names on the mailboxes we arrived at my Gramp's place to find him obviously dressed up for our visit in a new red and black plaid shirt that made his belly seem even bigger, cheeks and jowls a-stubble as usual, and with company. A long wagon with iron wheels, hitched to a pair of mules, stood in the driveway.

Two Amishmen stood by the wagon talking to Gramp; or, they nodded as he talked as we pulled in and got out of the car. The tall one wore a black cone-like hat, the short one a railroad cap. Both wore overalls and had whiskers that began just under the chin.

"W-well," bellowed Tom Northway as we walked to them, "it is the wanderers come home! You fellows know my boy Marcus, don't you? And his boy Bo? H-how are you, big boy? Let's see that muscle there—Why, you need to c-come out here on the farm with me, Bo, build yourself up, that's a chicken muscle!"

My father was shaking hands with Abel Miller and with Junior Zooks.

"You know Abel," Gramp declared, "helped to build this w-wonderful house—"

"Hello, Abel," Mark Northway said.

"Hello, Marcus," said Abel, who had known my father since when they were boys and Dad used to come to visit Uncle Ed and Aunt Gussie out here.

"And do you know Junior? He is a very famous checker player. Isn't that right, Junior? You have not been by just for a game in a long time. I was afraid you might be avoiding me for my h-halitosis."

Abel and Junior looked at each other, and at my father and me, with half-smiles on their faces, for Gramp was always joking them, and they appreciated it, out of their tradition though it was.

"How is Alma Mae?" I asked the taller, older man, her father.

"She is expecting a baby now, before long," he said.

"Please give her my best wishes."

The Amishman looked at me with eyes so expressionless I doubted it was a message that would be delivered. I had been "sweet on" Alma Mae, a girl my own age, visiting Gramp out here the summer before. I thought how strange that she was settled down now, married to a great block of an older man, and pregnant, sealed off from me. I would feel silly even writing her a letter.

"I'm glad you boys came by," Gramp said to his Amish friends. "That's a good idea, re-activating the old quarry, Abel. W-why, look at this fine house we built with that stone! You just take and do it! It is fine with me."

Abel nodded. He and the squat checker champion got on the wagon, nodded again. Abel gee-hawed and the mules clopped and the wagon rattled down the driveway to the road. Then Gramp embraced us; and his English bulldogs Jill and Jiggs came bounding up.

Arm in arm my father and his father walked towards the stone house Tom Northway and Abel Miller and some others here had built. Accompanied by the brute dogs I

walked around the place. The spring rains had been heavy.
The corn was growing tall. Everything was lush.

The little plot garden in the side yard was fenced round
with blacklocust poles and chickenwire. A tub sat full of
rainwater for watering by bucket. Alma Mae had planted
two rows of bright summer flowers for Gramp, whom she
adored. In the "tourist court" for chickens were Gramp's
Little Rhodies and White Leghorns. Nearby simmered a
great iron pot, full of meatleavings for them from Miller's
slaughterhouse; the air carried its smell of boiling meat and
hickory smoke. Beyond was the stand of sugar maples, and
back in the woods the 100-year-old syrup house.

I stopped by the old gas-engined circular saw worked
by pulleys where the locust, apple and sycamore logs were
sawed into short discs to be split down the middle for
burning. Gramp had taught me both those tasks, the
sawing and the handling of the doublebit ax, on my
summer visits here, as my father had taught me the work
around our smaller place. Gramp's pet milk goat, which in
one of his humors he had named Hubert de Burgh, came up
to me, dainty-footed. I rubbed her horny head, sorry I did
not have a Lucky Strike for her.

Now they had moved to the side porch. They seemed to
be having a heated conversation. It must be about Aunt
Ida's will. From the look of it I did not figure that Gramp
was going to do anything more about it than Harry was. I
thought I understood why. I didn't think it was because
Gramp had gotten unexpected money from the will. My
understanding of it was that Tom Northway, forced into a
profession, dentistry, he never really liked by Uncle Marcus,

had then spent his life getting away from the influence of Uncle Marcus and Aunt Ida and their money and fighting their imperialism towards his son. I could understand if he did not give a hoot about trying to get any more of their money now, especially at the price of an upsetting struggle. He had his place, and dear God, he loved it here on the farm, and had enough to keep it and to keep it going for as long as he would last. (Which proved to be another 20 years, my Gramp living to an age of more than 90 on his beloved farm place.)

But shouldn't he ought to do it, fight the will anyway, for his son's sake—just because it was so terribly unjust?

I stopped rubbing the goat's knobby head. Ought was a damn hard thing to figure.

I hesitated, then went to join them on the porch, hoping with all my heart they were not angry with each other.

As I sat down beside them on the porch, they were not talking about the will at all.

"Not to be trusted?" Dad was saying. "That's like saying don't invite a bear into your honey ranch. The Russians are mean as hell, bent on total domination of the world. Why, they haven't cooperated on anything since the war ended. They are the next ones we'll have to fight just because of their desire to expand their Godless system. That idea they came up with for the Five Year Plan was the only good thing the world ever got from the Russians!"

That year the Russians had taken over Czechoslovakia, then blockaded Berlin, and we were having to fly in food.

Tom Northway shook his head of unbridled white hair and changed the subject. He was heavier but shorter than his son. "What do you think of that fellow Stassen, Marcus?" he said. "He's pretty h-hot, isn't he? He might be all right, since poor old Taft, your illustrious neighbor there, will never make it. He is coming in here, to Burton and Washington Court House and all around, Stassen is, to campaign for the primary. I thought I might go see him, at Burton."

"Stassen—he's a liberal in disguise. A disguised Democrat is what that joker is."

"Well, maybe so. He makes some sense though. I may vote for him. He strikes me a lot like W-Wendell W-Wil—Goddamn it!—W-Wendell Willkie!"

"Now Dad, Stassen is about as much like Willkie as Abel Miller is. Did you enjoy your walk around, son?"

"Everything looks great, Gramp."

He nodded, pleased. Then he said: "Now I think of it, Marcus, I recall going to Washington Court House another time. That was to hear President Harding speak. That was after the time I shook his hand in the lobby of the Deschler Hotel, there in Columbus. Both times were before he was President. Old Harding, then, wasn't much more than a country-come-to-town. Some people thought he was a Negro."

"If so," my father said, "that was the least of his problems."

"And then, you know, the train with dead Harding on it passed through Newton Falls. I didn't go over there to see it, n-not as thrilled by the prospect of a dead president as some, but I remember Cousin Jake Northway, the same one who trained the carrier pigeons in W-World War One, and when asked as to the secret of his success with them said, 'W-why, you just have to know a little more than the pigeons,' he went over there. Jake was one of them put a half dollar on the track and the train flattened it. Was buried, I understand, Bo, with that half dollar, about what he had. That, and the damn pigeons, were the only things, of course, of interest that Jake ever did."

They laughed at the old story of Jake Northway and the pigeons, repeated so many times in family lore.

"What time is it getting to be?" Dad looked at his watch. The gesture seemed to say, it would be a long drive back. It made me sit up straight and look at him.

"Hey," I said, "I thought we were going to spend the night."

"Oh? Sure— That was the plan, wasn't it? I— Seems like we've been going a long time. It's hard to stop."

"Of course you're staying! You wouldn't treat an old farmer like that, would you? W-Why, I have a lovely evening planned for us! I have made some Irish ice cream that would do Dutch Potts proud! We'll eat that and wash it down with some marvelous bock beer that is the envy even of your mighty beer-producing P-Porkopolis, and I will tell Bo's fortune in the foam on the beer! Then I have planned a circus for you in the barn. Abel Miller and Junior Zooks have consented to do their famous dance- and-comedy routine, like Oakley and Buttner, and Jill and Jiggs here, why, they will do the Highland Fling! Then we will all s-speak a riddle or a piece!"

The "Irish ice cream" turned out to be hot corned beef and cabbage. After dinner, drinking a second of the heavy, almost black spring beers, I prevailed on Gramp to tell us one of the many stories he had created. Some he had haphazardly written down, some lived in his mind. This evening he told one of his "Forty Acres" tales, of the famous fight between the vicious dog Hobo and the great ram Slugger. I could tell Dad grew impatient as he told it.

"It always amazes me," he said when Gramp had finished, to my applause, "how you make that slow old ram whip a huge mongrel dog."

"Yes," Gramp said. "That is amazing, Marcus. That is because it is f-fiction. Most people, in life, would know better than to go after a dog with a ram."

It struck me that my grandfather was making a veiled reference to the will.

With me in the kitchen, as he and I washed the dishes and Dad sat smoking a Dutch Masters colorado on the porch just outside, Gramp said, "I hope your mother can talk him out of this—this crazy contesting of Ida's will! That would be foolish, you know—like going after a r-rainbow! Anyway, that poor pitiful woman, McAdoo, the nurse, why, she nursed Ida for years! There might be, Bo, though your father would never admit it, a case to be made that she deserves it, eh? Every G-Goddamn penny of it."

"You knew them, Gramp. What were they really like? Aunt Ida and the General? They did love Dad, didn't they?"

"Like? My God. He was a very proud man w-who in later life married a rich woman who almost immediately died, and then had the ill fortune to marry Ida. She was his first wife's nurse—did you know that? Is that what you great writers call po-poetic justice?" Gramp whacked a plate down on the counter, chuckling. "Though he did have things to be proud about all on his own, in his line of work, you'd have to admit. He invented a stretcher, you know." Now Gramp laughed fully, then said: "She was a terrible woman."

Putting his dish towel on its peg and letting the dogs and Hubert de Burgh into the house for the night, he said, in what he conceived to be a whisper, "Yes. They loved him, loved my boy. It almost killed Mattie, his own mother, how they loved our boy and how they tried to take him from us with material things. But your father was always a good boy, very loyal to his parents, and did what he had to do in that situation. Now, Bo, he should know that, having turned his back on them then, no matter what they said before, they would never really—Oh well! I w-wish, my very dear boy, I really do wish that he could just simply let it be water over the d-d-d—Goddamn—dam!"

Gramp's voice had gotten louder as he spoke.

"Are you cursing again, Dad?" my father said, with just a hint of a smile, coming in from outside behind the dogs and goat. "You are a terrible influence on my son."

Gramp slept upstairs in the big bedroom in the bed that had been his and Mattie's. The mastiffs slouched down to their basement pallets. We slept on cots in the living room, of which the kitchen was an extension. Full of the heavy beer I dreamed of Ruth and of lovely Alma Mae so prim and ripe for marriage the summer before, and of my California cousin in the mountains, all swirled together, and woke in black night discomfited. Tiptoeing to the door, I got it open and whizzed off the porch onto the orange and yellow flowers I could not name. It was a moonless night.

My father switched on the lamp beside him as I came back in. He had been sitting in his pajamas in one of the old black leather chairs.

"You okay?" he said.

"Yes. Are you? I'm sorry, that— They all—"

"Oh, you've got to know and appreciate, in this life, you can't always get others to do what you want them to. Right? It's 'no strain, no pain,' as you guys say. I understand, I guess, why they don't want to. But it was worth a try."

"What will you do about it now? The will?"

"I don't know, old boy. We'll just have to see. Maybe I'll decide to follow my true nature and be real sweet. Maybe I'll write McAdoo and that lawyer guy a letter of congratulations."

His glasses were off. There were deep creases where they went on his face above his cheeks.

"Your Gramp had this chair for many years when he was in the practice of dentistry in Cleveland," he said. "I remember it, the feel and the smell of it, real well. I remember that Dad was always scrubbed clean and smelled of peppermint then. And I remember—"

He stopped. The goat, curled up in a corner, stirred, opened a yellow eye at us, and shut it.

"Did you ever, really, know him very well?"

"Who, son?"

"The General."

"Oh, that's hard to say. At times I felt pretty close to him. Every time he appeared was an occasion."

He rubbed the bridge of his nose, put his glasses on, laughed softly to himself, his mood changing.

"I remember this one time—it was to be an important talk we would have about my future—when Ida and Uncle Marcus had gotten us all out to their place there in California, at Coronado. It was a gorgeous spread. My mother was there, and Dad, none too happy about it. And the day after we got settled in there the old boy had us, he and I, driven in to San Diego, to the zoo. And we walked, if you can believe it, around that zoo together and he pointed little lessons of nature and of life for me as we walked. Then we stopped in front of this big old lion—the poor thing was off its feed for the heat and just lying there in its cage—and with the King of the Beasts as a setting, he asked me what profession I was thinking of devoting my life to. It was Spring Break from Yale, which I hated, where they'd sent me. I was already twenty-one and just a freshman again there, at Yale."

He paused, smiling in his reminiscence. The lamplight played over the ceiling and cast a reflection back to the fireplace, the stone taken and cut from the "Edward Northway Quarry 1850–1880," as the plaque there told.

"Well, my dear son, he thought I'd say Law, or I suppose he even hoped Medicine, or something great and significant like that. Even Horticulture might have done, he had taken me to gawk at old Burbank the summer before, at Sebastopol there, Burbank's proving ground in California. So I said I was interested in following the great new creative force that was shaping and transforming America, by which I meant Advertising."

41

"What did he say to that?"

"Why, not much. His noble mug got the most—what?—puzzled look. As if he hardly knew what that was. But he was always kind, and interested, even later on by which time he must have come to think I was incorrigible. He was a strange duck, self-made completely, you see, and so a fierce old bird; but could be real gentle too, if you can feature that."

"Yes," I said, for of course I could.

Driving back home the next morning Dad said, "I guess not getting anything but chickenfeed of Ida's dough might make us all take a little more notice of what we're doing and where we're going, don't you think?"

"Sir?"

"Oh, I had built—foolishly, of course—some hopes, or dreams, around that damn inheritance. As if—And you, Bo. You too, son."

I looked over to where he was driving, face set, eyes straight on the road, to see what he meant exactly.

"You should be thinking for sure now that you will go to college. It would have been nice, and fun and rewarding and great experience I'm sure, to play Hemingway and just roam around and practice being a writer, but practically, son—"

I didn't want it to get grim. "You mean," I said, "I should be thinking of going to Harvard?"

He had to grin. "No," he said, "you don't have to go to Harvard."

"I'll go where you went, then."

"Well, you go where you want to go," he said. "I do think it would be a terrible risk, not to do it, but the choice of where you go is yours." He grinned again. "You might even want to go to Yale, and love the damn place."

Oh boy, I thought, there goes Paris. But I knew that he was right.

Later in the summer he went for a few days to Chicago, to see about a high-paying job in merchandising there. The wrangling with the television monster was getting to be a major strain on him.

"Oh, he won't take that job, even if they're really interested in him," Mom said. "He loves this place of ours, and Ohio, too much. But it's so good for him right now to have another possibility. Do you ever smoke?"

She was curled up on the couch while I sat in an old chair in the den room downstairs, the same couch Ruth and I would sometimes "make out" on (the most proper, old-fashioned "making out" imaginable, as I recall it now) when we thought they were all asleep upstairs. The room held the upright piano on which Dad would on rare occasions belt out "Roll Out the Barrel" and the 11-inch Crosley TV set that was now the dominating Cyclops in our life. Now it was off. Smoke curled from Mom's cigaret in the lamplight. We could hear the sounds of summer in the night air outside, and every once in a while the scratch of a Miller moth on the window screen. Both Joy and Luke were off spending the night with friends.

"No. I tried rolling some Bull Durham cigs with Wolf. It was a mess. None of us guys smokes."

"My Goodness, how the men in my family smoked! I remember the Whitlock men, at the old house out in the country, sitting on the porch after dinner with their cigars."

"I'll give it a go, Mom."

"No. I do enough for all of us."

"How do you think he is? He still seems down about it. He comes home every night, you guard him from us, so he can take a nap—"

"I need to," she snapped. "He needs rest. He's having trouble at the office—policy and people problems. Anyway, I think he has decided not to contest that silly will. Or, he's let it go by so it's too late now. He called his sister, your Aunt Lellie, in Philadelphia. The last link, the last base untouched, as he would say. They've been estranged. Lellie didn't seem to know what in the world he could be talking about, she was no more aid or comfort than Harry or Gramp. 'It is true you were always Ida's favorite,' she said. She reminded him that Ida and the General had spent quite a bit of money sending him to Yale and all before he rebelled from them, and had never spent a penny on her. (They would have, though. They offered her a trip to Europe to get out of the clutches of your Uncle Morrie, but she happened to love him and married him instead.) Lellie asked him if he was going up to that auction next month, in Greenwich. At Willowstone, Marcus and Ida's estate there. They are going to auction off all that gorgeous stuff, from there and from the other houses. We have the auction catalogue. It's incredible."

"Did all that go to Nurse McAdoo too?"

"Sure. Your father, of course, says he won't go up there if his life depends on it. I am trying hard to get him to go. I think he should. I think it might do him good, clear his mind."

"Why?"

She gave me a hard, blue-eyed look, tamped her cigaret and fetched another from the pack.

"Because he would be doing something. He'd see the old place, that Willowstone, as it really is. A grim, dull place. And maybe he could get something he remembers or really wants, even if he did have to buy it."

"That would be a funny use of the money he did get from the will."

She gave me a strange look, as if I might be closing in on adulthood, then said: "Yes. It would. How about a beer?"

In our state they had 3.2 beer, which parents thought couldn't hurt kids much. She went to the kitchen and got two ice cold Hudepohls, set one down for each of us, then went up the stairs to their room, and came back with the auction catalogue. She settled herself back down and turned the pages of the prospectus.

"All this stuff! You can't imagine. Some of it I've seen, and remember—From all over the world. Almost every year they took a trip—"

She flipped the gray, dull-looking pamphlet to me. Slowly I looked through it. There were more than 100 pages of catalogued items, single-spaced.

Linens. China. Crystal. Silver. Furniture. Rugs. Paintings.

Aristex. Hepplewhite. San Domingo mahogany. Royal Worcester. Capo di Monte. Italian Rose Point de Venice. Carved ivory. Bokharas and Shivrans.

"Boy," I said, "I never even heard of half this stuff. How about this? 'Old Princess Bokhara, elephant foot print in ruby field.'"

"Oh, I remember that. That was in Ida's bedroom for years."

"Now the nurse's foot has covered up the elephant's." I flipped the catalogue back to her.

"Hah," she said, and read: "'Oriental hand-carved tiered Buddhist temple in fine detail. Steps lead to the first cubicle. Doors open to reveal an idol. This is roofed and at each of the four corners is hung a small bell. Another room surmounts this. This repeated for five levels in graduated effect.' 'Surmounts.' Oh, I do like that. My Goodness, I am so sorry not to be getting that, for the mantel in the living room!"

She passed it back. In a moment I said: "Here, this would be even better for the mantel. 'The Dream. Oil on porcelain in gilt frame. A maiden is shown reclining on a snow-covered peak. Her right arm is flung above her head as if in sleep. On a ledge below her two girls are seated. One is dressed in a softly draping blue net, a star adorning her hair and in her left hand is a cluster of flowers. The other is similarly attired but in a gown of yellow hue—' Woo, woo, yellow hue! '—which falls to her shoulders to reveal—' Hold it! '—her bosom. In the background are the sky and stars.'"

We laughed.

46

"Gosh, Bo, it was another world. Not ours, surely. Just think of it, collecting, having it all—"

She took back the dun-colored booklet one more time.

"I remember this, I truly do, so well. Uncle Marcus sitting at it, Bo, so stern and fine and proud. Not just in pictures but in person, there in his paneled study, not at Willowstone, but in the suite at the Waldorf where actually they—he anyway—mostly stayed. If your father sees this, and it's available, and doesn't cost an arm and a leg, as he would say, maybe this is what he would want to get, want to have. Listen to this, Bo: 'Custom made, English. Block front, knee-hole flat top desk. Double central drawer and graduated end drawers, both front and back. On fluted and shaped legs. Figured mahogany veneers of rare beauty. B. Altman, New York.' That was the General's writing desk, for all those years, in that apartment at the Waldorf. I'm sure our guy would like to have that, and to pass it on to you."

But actually Dad's cousin Harry bought that desk of the General's at the auction up there, and put it in his lawyer's office. And of course my father did not go up there to bid on anything that should by rights be his anyway. And we all understood why without anything being said about it. We never really thought he would. We understood that it was the principle of the thing.

GRADUATION

That year my father's career ceased to follow an ascending arc and began to take on a zigzag, up and down and back and forth, character that continued for the rest of his active life.

I do not know whether he was demoted, or "promoted sideways" or simply moved like a pawn on the chessboard at the great clear-channel station; but he found himself taken out of "the television end of things" with the coming of the coaxial cable and an experienced hotshot from New York put in charge of the TV enterprise. At the same time the local newspaper did a story on him, and he received a plaque from the station hailing him as a "television pioneer," an honor I am not sure pleased him all that much. He was moved back over into sales and merchandising, and I don't think his vice-presidency continued with the move. There was a young fellow whom Dad had hired in the first place, before taking over the inchoate TV monster, and whom he liked a lot who had already been made the VP for that line of things, a fellow by the name of Ronald Cross.

I remember, thinking of my father and the station, a "party" Mom and Dad threw in the spring of that year in the face of what was happening. I think it was my mother's idea, to cheer him up. He had finally warmed to the idea, but in a way quite characteristic of him.

"I know you'd like to check on how it's going," Ruth said after we had been to our movie. "It's fine with me, Bo. Let's."

We drove back up to the Hill and along Miami Run and our own Shawnee Run, and in our driveway. They had said we were welcome to come by and say hello. I knew they meant they hoped we would.

It was a bad, wet spring. Light shone through the drizzle from the windows of our house. Half a dozen cars were parked from the house to the old half-painted barn behind. I thought of pulling over on the yard, under the line of apple trees, but that might make tire ruts in the grass. We parked the Plymouth behind someone's Lincoln Zephyr.

The whole notion of the party for the people from the station had been ruined by the rain. Everyone was in the gameroom at the back of the barn, where heavy, greasy-black machines of some sort had been when we moved in. Dad had gotten up his enthusiasm about having this party, but strictly in his own way. He and my mother almost never entertained; he hated to entertain formally, with cocktails and such nonsense. Everyone was to come to the party informally, that is, specifically, in lumberjack clothes. There would be—shades of his farmer father, Tom Northway! —an old-fashioned wood-chopping contest and other rustic games. Bobbing for apples for all I knew. Dad would "throw some chickens on the grille," barbecue them on the great stone grille he'd built on the terrace beside the house on which he cooked with splits of flaring apple and black locust and hickory, not your damn charcoal. It would be an outdoor party, under the yellow, moth-encrusted terrace and barn lights. He had a square-dance record, and would call it.

Thunder rumbled gently from far away over the Kentucky hills across the river as Ruth and I walked down the lighted path by the toolshed and the privy to the barn. One of Mom's instructions from him had been to get the old stinking two-holer as sweet smelling as possible. How she followed that instruction I never knew.

We eased in to the old game room where for years we'd had family ping-pong, high school parties, and barn dances after football games.

We beheld about a dozen people there of various types and ages and in various stages of inertia. Mostly they just stood around in the big barn room, unfocused. No one, obviously, was having any fun. It wrenched my heart.

My father, dressed in a red and black plaid shirt and his baggy khakis, with his doublebit ax in his hands as symbol of the myth of what the evening was meant to be, moved

51

from knot to knot of people. In one corner obvious station executives and their wives who had missed the signal and were suited up and in party dresses stood and talked, holding cups of cider and highball glasses. Dad must have relented and produced the bottle of Old Granddad and the Bottle of Dewars White Label which sat usually unused in the liquor cabinet in the house. Hoppy, Dad's short fat obnoxious hillbilly assistant at the station, was the only one dancing. He was jigging around with someone's wife, a stout woman who wore a tight black silk dress. Someone had put on Vaughn Monroe singing "Dance, Ballerina, Dance" in that wonderful deep voice he had because he had a mole in his throat. It did not fit Hoppy or his stout partner very well. But Hoppy at least had taken the invitation seriously; he wore blue jeans and the cap Dad despised; yet his costume, plus his antic dancing, seemed to consciously mock what my father had envisioned. Standing alone with his wife in a corner I recognized Bill Schwarzkopf, a tall silver-haired man from an old family in the city who was executive vice-president at the station. My father had many a fight over TV programming with him before being moved aside. Schwarzkopf looked bored. His tall, silver-haired wife looked to be the coolest one in the barny room, an interesting phenomenon considering she seemed to have wrapped herself in a Shetland blanket.

It was an odd crowd of people brought together. Hans and Emily Verinder, our Swiss next-door neighbors, sat at the redwood table, drinking pop. Dad, who had absolutely no belief that "good fences make good neighbors," had been so offended when Hans built his rose-covered picket

fence along his property line that I was amazed he had let
Mom invite them. I wondered if he had spoken to Hans.
My favorite teacher Ben Stockwell, an electric- haired
dynamo from the East, and his wife were talking to some
foreign students from the university, some of the students
Mom contacted through her Club and had to dinner from
time to time. These were Oriental guys who nodded and
smiled and nodded. I saw Mr. Ash from my school, but
could not believe what I was seeing: my English teacher
stood swaying from side to side, red-faced with a very dark
glass of something in his hand, declaiming poetry or
something to my buddy Jake Stillman's mother, who wrote
poetry herself when not stirring up causes on the Hill. Mr.
Ash, to my amazement, appeared to be smashed.

My brother Luke and his friend Denny sat at the end of
the red-checker-clothed table, eating beans and chicken.
No one else seemed to have been drawn to the food. Dad
had hoped that some of the musical talent from the station
might appear and entertain ex tempore, but none had made
it. Now the rain beat down harder on the roof, and I saw
Mom dash out towards the house to do or to get something.
I saw the effort she'd put out. Obviously she'd had to cook
and fix it all in the house and bring it out here, the chicken,
beans, salad, rolls, and chocolate cake, made always a little
soggy because that was how he liked it. My mother looked
hot-faced and lovely-sad, kind of like Gene Tierney, in her
jeans and checkered shirt with sleeves rolled up. Joy must
be in the house, gone to bed or just escaped. Ruth let go of
my hand to put her damp raincoat back over her shoulders
and followed Mom into the house.

Dad, whose face never under any circumstances was capable of forced joviality, came to greet me gravely and led me over to pay my respects to Bill Schwarzkopf and his wife. He told me his son had gone to Deerfield and was now at Harvard. I nodded at him like that was peachy keen. Then Dan introduced me to Ronald Cross. Instinctively I liked him, usurper that he was. He was fairly young with a real smile, and had worn old clothes. His pretty wife wore slacks.

Vaughn Monroe kept singing, but no one danced. I saw Hoppy pouring out the last of the bourbon into his glass and taking a gulp of it. A fire flamed and hissed in the black pot-bellied stove, making it too hot in the dark, yellow-lit old game room.

Before long, then, everyone left the party. I keep this image of my father going out the barn door in his old clothes with a tall Sikh in a turban and two small Chinese guys, to drive them back to the university: in that moment in his red-plaid shirt and ill-fitting khakis and floppy hat, setting his ax against the wall, he looked like a comic figure on a stage, like the country Yankee come to town in the Royall Tyler play.

"Thanks so much, Ruth dear," Mom said, her eyes clouded. "Will you kids lock up when you leave, and make sure the fire's banked?"

"I think we're leaving—" I said.

"Good night. See you in the morning."

Sitting parked in the Plymouth in Ruth's driveway in the rain, we held on to each other for a long time. Then Ruth said, "Do you know something? You Northways think you're so terribly special, and you're really not."

It made me angry.

"Daddy says, oh, that you'll think I'm not good enough for you when you go off to college, and I have to stay here and work. He says that you're a wanderer anyway."

Ruth's father had a peculiar way of being right about things, considering that he was "retired" and spent his time gardening or playing the violin attired in a silk dressing gown. Ruth's mother was a spunky character. She worked, as Ruth had also since she was 15.

"And do you know what Mother says? She says it's too bad you're not Jesus, but you're not."

Piqued as I was, I had to laugh at that.

Jesus or not, I had a golden senior year. Turned 18, I seemed invincible. I wrote the California story, finding it was more about the courage of my grandparents, Luke and Remember Whitlock, going out there at their age to make a new start than about my feverish first love. My English teacher, Mr. Ash, at his soberest said he thought that it showed promise. Digging around that spring in the family stuff I found a small diary of the year 1866 that had been kept by my great-grandfather Elijah Northway as he did the simple tasks on the farm up there in Geauga County while courting a young schoolteacher. This was after he came back from being released from a Confederate prison camp in Texas when the war ended. I began my second story, making up the story of the battle he'd been captured in, though nothing of that was mentioned in the diary. It was my first journey into research and imagination.

In less important matters, I wrote idealistic editorials for the school paper. ("The school of life will knock some of those ideas out of your head," my father said. "Who do you think you are, old Emerson?") In fall football I made a famous tackle of the county champions' star running back, knocking him out cold in the middle of the field. I simply put my arms up as he ran at me, wishing he would swerve around me, and actually was sorry. One of the school Trustees cautioned my father about this streak of violence in me. "He's very gentle around the house," my father said. Through that year Ruth and I "went steady," so very steady that it seemed to everyone, including us, that we were married. She was a sympathetic, loving person who had dreams and who could, though sometimes sadly, sit and listen to my own. And we stayed "pure." We guarded her as if her destiny was to be the Virgin to be sacrificed at the highest altar.

My buddy Jake Stillman and I, with Ben and Mr. Ash behind us, decided to go off to college the next year, and to go to the small liberal arts college which, after the charade of Yale, my father had chosen as the place where he could be his own person, his father's son and not the ward and foster son of General Marcus.

And so the year spun around to when the length of summer and all new opportunity lay just beyond the tender springtime, and there came my day of graduation from the school on the Hill.

I awoke on that day, the window of my room in our old farmhouse open, "rosy-fingered dawn" at play outside, the odors of fields and flowers coming in, knowing surely that

56

this was, would be, my most significant day. And woke feeling the strong hand of my father upon my shoulder, now gently shaking me.

I sat up. He stepped back. I looked at him. He had on his flannel shirt, his old work clothes.

"Hey," he said, "are you going to sleep your life away?"

"I'm awake."

"It's nearly eight," he said. "I thought you would want to get up, today."

He moved to the door. I remember the bagginess of his pants, how his frayed belt missed half the loops, the softness and earth-look of his flannel shirt, the eagerness there was in his eyes every single morning to get out and get at it. "Look to this day, for it is life, the very life of life . . . " My mother, lover of poetry, recited it; but it was my father who was always there to greet the dawn.

In the doorway he stopped, turned back and smiled. "I'm proud of you," he said. "Oh, it's not the grades you've made, or any awards you may get today from the school. You have been, to your mother and me, a satisfactory son."

"Satisfactory." The sentimentalist's objectification of emotions that ran so deep that it would be foolish, corny, unmanly to try to voice them in any but an understated way.

He pinched the bridge of his nose, adjusted his specs, and said, now gruffly, "We are all going to have breakfast, I'm told, outside on the terrace after a while. After that I don't see why we shouldn't get a few things accomplished around here today, do you?"

I looked at him. Saturday was "work day" around the place, but . . .

57

"But it's your day, son. You do what you want to do. Okay?"

Okay. We would mow and hoe and God knew what. The ritual of the cultivation of the Garden would go on. To him if this was a special, a significant, day it should be marked by doing something useful. The graduation ceremony at the school was not until the evening.

I looked to see the present he—my parents—had already given me sitting on my dresser, a gleaming new portable typewriter. I was to go downtown to a business college this summer and learn to type professionally. If I would not get out and learn carpentry or how to lay bricks I could at least do that, learn to use this tool like a pro and not a random pecker at the keys—to master it, learn to compose on it, quit scrawling on my Big Chief pads, and thus save time and improve the powers of concentration and organization. That is, if writing was going to be my line.

I got up, flexed my "chicken muscles," winked at myself in the mirror and went down the hallway to the bathroom. Joy was sound asleep in her room and through brother Luke's closed door I could hear him snoring so loudly that I knew he thought I was Dad returning and was faking it.

Dressed, I found my mother and her mother in the kitchen. Luke and Remember had been invited and, I suspected, financed by my father in coming for this rite of passage. They were sleeping in the game room of the barn. They had taken the City of San Francisco to Chicago, then arrived here two days ago on the James Whitcomb Riley. My other grandfather, Tom Northway, was also here, on a cot in the little study called the "memorial" room, where, he said, all the images of the old General and his friends on the walls gave him claustrophobia, not to mention a "p-pain in the ass." "To celebrate our dear boy's graduation, why don't we have a nice b-bonfire and burn all these damn old p-pictures?" he said to my father.

"Do you remember, Louise," my grandmother was saying to Mom, "out at the old place, the Hathaway homeplace, when you were very young, how your grandmother and I would prepare breakfast for the men? Eggs and bacon and ham, Gracious, fried potatoes and apple pie? Those men never thought they had eaten breakfast unless they had apple pie. And your grandfather, my father Milo, and his hands would come in to eat it about seven o'clock? They'd been up milking, working, since four-thirty. They really farmed the place then, you know."

I went to embrace her, this white-haired little woman not more than five feet high who had married her lanky six-foot-six man, this strongest, sternest, most critical, and serenest member of our family. The lore said once she had been courted by the crazy poet Vachel Lindsay, chanting his mad Boomlay poems to her on the long porch of the homestead of the startled Hathaways.

"Ah! My Beau," she said, briskly kissing me.

She had told me in her stern mystical manner, that time in California, letting go my palm-up hand, that though I was born half-blind I was to be lucky through life, that with effort and perseverance I would make it through to my "heart's desire." Now I call her back: hair softly white but vibrant; eyes blue, and either paling to ice or the blue of flame; a passionate person, I do think; who would tell you your destiny or switch you for your transgressions, always calling for the best in you. Cocking her head, so small, fierce as a sparrow.

"We'll have a big breakfast late, about ten, if you can last," my mother said.

"Complete with apple pie?"

Remember laughed, putting "cuckoo bread" into the oven. And seeing her in the kitchen a flash came to me of being much younger—five or six—and waking suddenly in the night when we were all except my father living some months on that island off Florida for my mother's arthritis and seeing her sitting by a candle in the one room in the cottage where we all slept: sitting bolt upright and watchful with a broom, guarding us from rats.

I went out on the front porch of the old house, which looked down a long sweep of grass to the tall hedge in front and, at the sides, the apple orchard and Hans Verinder's white-painted fence. Gramp Tom, all plaid belly and bristly jowls and old straw hat, and Grandpa Luke, all long lines of legs and points of elbows and thatch of white but boyish hair, both bright blue-eyed and emitting an electric vitality in the enjoyment of being with each other, were sitting in rockers in the morning sunshine drinking coffee and smoking Luckies. We'd had a big game of Hi Low Jack and the Game the night before, with Ruth sitting in the family circle, until Tom Northway, because he was not winning, had thrown down his cards and retired, saying, "No one's having any f-fun!" Luke Whitlock, who had pulled in most of the pots, gave us all a wink at that. Now he sat, the skinny hand with the cigaret in it cocked out beside, the cigaret burning down to a nub, that fresh look in his Lincolnesque face as if each encounter was a wonder.

"Well, Bo," he said. "Doctor here and I were just discussing what a phenomenon of a student you have become." His voice had a slow, soft-timbred, Indiana tone, where Gramp was all Ohio brass, whether it came out baritone or bass or however he chose to flugle it at you. "We're mighty proud of our boy today."

"Well," Gramp Tom said, flying his own burning shred of cigaret over the porch rail, "we said we were not going to say so, Luke. Bo's m-many admirable qualities sometimes do not include modesty."

"Let's just say he has come a long way then, Tom. Eh? Done all right with what was provided."

"Yes. I w-would hardly have imagined it, his rise to such schoolboy f-fame and glory, would you, Luke? Remembering, that is, when we first beheld him?"

"That's right, Tom. Right as rain. I'm afraid we had our doubts, Bo. Your grandfathers came down, you know, arm in arm up there in Cleveland to the hospital, in Shaker, you know, after we had stopped to fortify ourselves at— Where was it, Tom?"

"Dutch's."

"Was it, Tom? I was thinking it was McGillicuddy's."

"Dutch's, Luke, no d-doubt about it."

"To see you, Bo, in your tiny incubator there, after they said it looked like you might really make it and stay with us in the world a while. You may not recall, or only from hearsay, but you kind of surprised us, in your importunate arrival, and caused some small concern, then and later—"

I had heard this story from them many times in the years of my growing up. I knew it was the story I wanted to hear from them today.

"Before that, b-before we were invited down there to view this wonder of wonders, you recall—"

"Of course, Tom. Your father, Bo, was off, down in Akron, I believe, interviewing desperately for a job he'd heard about. It was the Depression, we'd lost everything we had in the family, all mine when the banks failed, Doctor here in the stock market—"

"You may skip that part, Luke."

"—and your father's advertising agency that he had started just out of college had gone under, and he was selling brassware from house to house, and so went to Akron because he heard there was a real sales job there with one of the big rubber companies. And when you were born so early and unexpected, and we reached him where he was staying he came roaring back, riding the rails—"

"H-hopped a freight, Bo, your father did, the first I believe since Si Northway to do so—though it was a common practice of old Si's."

"And came roaring into the hospital and found the doctor who had delivered you, runt that you were, and in the hallway there that doctor told him, 'You have a son, Mr. Northway, but don't bother to name him, for he isn't going to live.'"

"And Marcus, your father, my boy, he says to that damn fool doctor, 'The hell he isn't!' and knocks that fellow down right there in the hallway of the hospital! And went in and with your dear mother he named you for himself, just to be c-certain of it."

"Is that true, Gramp? Luke? It's a good story—but did he really knock him down, the doctor?"

"Why don't you ask him?" Tom Northway said. I shrugged.

"It's as true as anything I know, Bo," said Luke Whitlock.

He fished a weed from the crumpled green-dot pack and bent way over sideways to take a light from Gramp's new fag. "So anyway, we got the green light, and got all dressed up, you know, in spats and top hats for the occasion—that was many years, as you know, before Doctor here had moved out yonder on the farm where he now scrapes the chickenshit off his overalls for special occasions, he was a real nice-looking, well-dressed fellow in those days—and we went in the hospital there and peered at what there was of you through the glass."

"After he had g-goggled at you for a while, r-rendered speechless by the sight, your grandfather Luke here, Bo, he says, 'W-why, Tom, I do believe he looks just like you.'"

Luke chuckled, then gasped as he inhaled and coughed a low rattly cough in his chest.

"'No, Luke,'" he said, recovering, "Tom says, 'I do believe he is the spit'n image of you.'"

"Then we both contemplated this red-faced little r-runt a while longer, and Luke says—"

"It was you said it, Tom."

"I distinctly recall, it was Dutch's, and you h-had a shot of good old Cincinnati Rittenhouse Rye, Luke, and it was you came out with it, standing there looking at him through

63

the glass, I am much too refined and of too n-noble a nature to have said it, 'W-well, w-what he actually looks like is a little Bo-hunk.'"

"So that was how you got your nickname, Bo. 'Little Bo-hunky' we called you then for years."

"I'd be grateful if you didn't call me that tonight, Grandpa."

"You have my word of honor, sir," said the judge.

"Now he devours books, and writes stories that put Rider Haggard to shame, and trips the light fantastic with a lovely girl who blushes every time he looks at her, and is going off to college in the f-fall. I'm not sure about your going to college there where your dad and Harry went, since I never observed that it did either of them much good. Your father just learned to make whiskey there in a still they had—now that was Prohibition time—and Harry got more ignorant, if anything, but that is your decision to make. You know I think you should come out to the farm with me, and l-let God Nature be your teacher, and learn all the lore and wisdom you will ever need, and j-just simply get to work writing, if that is what you want to do. Anyway, you are a fortunate boy, no one is making you go to Ya- Ya-Goddamn it!—Yale!"

I left them smoking, laughing and talking—thinking that if I stayed with them I'd remember my graduation day as when I took up cigaret smoking and coffee drinking—and walked down the front steps by the big ash tree and around the house by the barn and to the tall field of sweetcorn, and other planted fields, towards the woods. I wondered where my father was, then saw him outside the fence of the chickenyard and run, dumping bushels of ripe tomatoes over to the birds. I ducked into the cornfield and went smoothly (like an Indian) through its saluting silky tassels. I wanted to be alone for a moment at the beginning of this special day. The sun was climbing the sky but was prisoner to clouds, making the day already slow of air and muggy as the sun pierced through the gray bands of cloud.

Through the corn I walked over what had been our large strawberry patch. Last year the guy who came to plow by mistake plowed all the strawberry plants under. Dad never was so mad, except when Verinder built that fence. Roses grew prettily on the fence now, but Dad never gave them reality by noticing them, never admitting they, or fence, were there. Through the tangle of woods, with their Tarzan vines, grew the blackberries Luke and I used to pick in quart buckets and try to sell from a wooden stand to people in cars passing by the house in front of the hedge. The profit was small and the price was poison ivy. Here now, up in this old oak tree which once had seemed so high, sat the plank treehouse my father's hands had built and to which I used to retreat when we had first moved here. Feeling mystically akin to it, and to the land, I felt its rough, edged bark, listened to the spring voice of the wind in its branches. I looked up to where two years ago, an eon ago, I had sat with Ruth and talked of my hopes, my being a "writer," our "future." Standing there I did what all boys who suddenly are not boys and have the grace of such a moment to reflect have done: went inward to myself, wondering at my 'selves,' wondering about self and soul and goal, Hero paused and poised, looking to the treehouse and up to the gray, blue sky, relinquishing the blackberry, treehouse boy I would never be again; before I turned and walked back through the woods and fields to my fathers, to my family.

I sat by Grandpa Luke and Remember and my sister Joy on a bench pulled to the redwood table on the terrace beside the house, across from Mom and Dad and Gramp and my brother Luke. Dad put his arm around his father's shoulder as Mom was snapping pictures of the occasion before she and Joy brought out the feast. No pie, but Mom's famous "cuckoo bread," hot and loaded with cinnamon and sugar; platters of ham and scrambled eggs; toast and jelly from the grapes on the arbor I could see just beyond the terrace; melon, milk and coffee.

"There's enough food here," Gramp boomed, making a well- known family pronouncement, "for the whole Rooshian Army!"

"So how about we eat it before they get here," said my brother Luke, with a look at our militantly anti-Communist father.

"Will you say a blessing, Mark?" my mother said, flushed from the kitchen and her travels to it, and now from the too-moist heat of a June mid-morning.

My father prayed briefly, in a one-two-three progression: for blessings, and especially for special blessings as on this day, thanks; of obligations and responsibilities, remind us; if Thy will be somehow clear, we'll try to do it. He, with some theology left, a blend of Methodist, Campbellite, and the mystic Fox, prayed to Our Father, in his version of the prayer of Jesus. My Gramp, Tom Northway, the farmerpantheist, always addressed the Great Father of Us All. My mother prayed, as she wrote her poetry, in her closet. We children preferred to stay in our closets, too, as we tried to sort out our fuzzy-edged beliefs.

When he was finished, and all but Luke had bowed his head, my mother and Remember said, "Amen."

Then Remember immediately said to my brother Luke: "Stop wiggling your foot. I believe it's bigger than your grandpa's. You are stirring up enough wind to blow the food away. If you need exercise, excuse yourself and take a quick walk around the house."

Luckily Luke was in a good mood, happy for me, not jealous of my "day." He would have gotten up and huffed off if anyone else—our father—had said such a thing to him, maybe started stalk-legging it around the house just to show us; but he smiled at Remember and made a great show of beholding and calming his size 12.

"Are these your own eggs, Marcus?" Gramp Tom said, shovelling in a forkful. "They are pretty good, but I still hold that my Little Rhodies outproduce, and form better eggs, than your L-leghorns. Do you raise anything out there in California by now, Luke?"

"No," said Grandpa Luke, sitting before his plate, barely touching it, a foot higher than anyone at the table, with a smile on his long lined face that seemed the essence of calm and contentment. "We have a small place, Tom. I pole a few beans, have a few Beefsteak tomatoes in a patch out back, is all. And Remember likes the sweet bell peppers. A kind called California Wonders do well there, and are pretty too."

"The Whitlocks were never the farmers the Northways are, or the Hathaways were," Remember said.

"W-won't you have some cuckoo bread, Luke?" Tom Northway said, to please the women. "It is delicious."

"Golly no, Tom. I've already eaten more than I usually do. Usually I have a bowl of mush in the morning, not much lunch, then Remember and I like a fish or veal dish for dinner."

"And too much coffee and too many cigarets on an empty stomach all through the day," Remember said.

Her husband smiled sheepishly at her, then turned his head to wink at me.

My father sat patiently over his second "cup of Joe," happy with this meal, this gathering, this ritualistic "family time." The talk turned to what was being worn to the graduation that evening and at what times I and the others should go, and in what cars. After a time of letting it roll on, Dad crushed out his lingering Spud and got up from the table.

"Time's a-wasting," he said heartily. "Joy, you can help your mother and grandmother with the dishes. We guys have a few things to get done around here."

"Oh Mark," my mother said, "let's not push today. Couldn't we call a moratorium today? I thought that in a while we might take Tom and Daddy and Mother on a drive around the Hill. The flowers are so lovely now."

"I'm not pushing. I just had in mind—Luke hasn't kept that field mowed, I've told him a hundred times, it's rank. Nothing heavy, Mother. We have to water the stuff anyway, get the old bucket brigade to going. But nobody else has to work, of course—"

"I'm coming, Mom," Joy said. Then, trying to joke, "I love to help with the dishes, except I'm afraid of getting dishpan hands!"

"Well," Mom said, flashing Dad a look, going beyond her usual public meekness. "I think—"

"It is very hot," Remember cut in tartly, "and humid. I had forgotten how terribly humid it is in the Ohio Valley."

"W-well, count me out," Gramp Tom said, standing, stretching, patting his full protruded belly, putting his hat rakishly on the back of his head. "I certainly did not come down here from the farm, you know, to work. After this fine meal, I think I will go and take a snooze."

He heaved up to the porch, to sit and watch whatever fools were going to work. I was just as glad. Last time he was here Gramp had tried to show my father the proper way to use the splitting maul.

"What can I do to help, Mark?" said Grandpa Luke, rising from the table, smoking, his long arms akimbo.

Dad smiled. Someone at least was going to stir his stumps, get in the work pattern with him.

"We've been waiting for someone of your rare height and ability to take a run at trimming that front hedge," he said.

"Fine. A little exercise would suit me. I can't ever remember sitting still so long. Can you imagine your old Grandpa in that Pullman booth, Bo?"

"'You're a poet and don't know it, 'cause your feet are Longfellows,'" I said, giving him back one of the endless lines he'd thrown at us when we were children.

"'Had an old horse and his name was Na-pol-ean, called him that because of his bony parts,'" he replied.

"You wait a while, Luke, until you have digested your breakfast," Remember said to him.

Grandpa Luke and I laughed. Remember was a fanatic on not drinking water with meals, chewing each mouthful of food 28 times, taking ten deep breaths to clear the lungs each time you went outside, and not reading while on the pot because it would give you piles. "Did, too," Grandpa Luke had whispered to me years ago.

"Bo, my dear Beau, sit with me and talk a minute," my grandmother said, as my brother Luke went to the barn to get the mower and Dad led my grandfather Luke, half a foot taller than he was, walking with his shambling gait, to the toolshed to get the shears with which to attack the high front hedge. "Tell me about that girl of yours. She's nice but awfully quiet, isn't she? Is she graduating from her school too?"

"No. She has another year to go."

"Will you keep up the romance, now you're going off to college?"

"'One never knows, do one?'" I said, affecting Fats Waller to fob off the question. My grandmother was terribly direct and to the point.

But she moved on to other things. She asked me if I still liked Dickens. She had grown up on Dickens, her father Milo Hathaway had read them Dickens sitting in the family circle at the old farmplace. Now her memories of growing up there kept filling her mind, as I doubtless would remember later in my life my own growing up time on these acres my father had found and claimed for us.

"It's odd," she said, "you must know, my dear, to have moved so far away at our age. I hope you will remember and cherish your roots—I know you will—your family and where you came from. As I do now, grown older. It was so peaceful growing up there, so lovely."

"I thought it was beautiful where you are now."

"San Berdoo? Oh yes. It is."

"Why exactly did you move out there?"

"You know we lost most of what we had, in the Thirties. No need crying over that, but your grandfather never quite made what they call a 'come-back' in Cleveland. He ran for office, you know—So during the War they allowed some civilians into the Judge Advocate's office of the Army Air Force, and Luke was flattered at the offer, and we decided to take it, go west and start again. And I am very proud of him. Now they have decided that civilians can serve as judge advocates of all those claims, and he has been asked to be the first one, and will become Judge Advocate over all of California and Arizona and Nevada next month."

"Hey! Why didn't he tell us?"

"Oh, you know how he is. But you can be sure I am going to inform your father. He has thought, at times in the past, that my man was lazy." Her eyes blazed. "Of course, he has always been very kind and helpful too." She paused, patted my hands folded before me on the redwood table, my skin beginning to feel the sun. "Yes. It is lovely where

71

we are, and especially up further, in the hills. And Luke loves that, as you know, the streams, the good trout fishing."

I laughed. "When he took me, he got so excited he threw down his rod and chased a fish down by a rock, and reached in and caught it in his hands!"

"And then let it go, I suppose?"

"Oh no. He put it in the creel, and we brought it home, remember? 'We won't tell your grandmother the exact circumstances of how we caught this beauty, will we?' he said."

She laughed. "I'll let you go," she said. "You go help your grandpa. He shouldn't exert so soon after eating. I'm glad you still like Dickens. It shows you have both literary and human sense. What a cast of characters—Heep and Barkus and Fagin and Micawber. I see them all around me every day! You will find all the characters you will ever need for your own writing right in this family. I have always marvelled at your father, how he needs to be doing something every minute. It's true that my Luke is different from that. He could sit for days and just look at a rushing stream under a blue sky. Isn't it funny that my other daughter married such a man as your father too? Why, when they came to visit us in California your Uncle Pete was up at dawn every day looking for something to do. He fixed our shutters, and painted the back part of the house that Luke had left for later, and he washed his car, and then washed our poor old car three times while they were with us that one week. Oh my. It interests me, my dear, how the Good Lord hands out talents and energies so variously."

Dad had taken the tractor over from my brother, who was filling buckets with water from the well pump and lugging them to the rows of tomatoes and other plants.

Tom Northway waved his hand at me from the porch, a cavalier gesture. He looked like a big bullfrog sitting there.

I walked down the slope of the long grassy lawn where I'd kicked the football or fungoed the softball over the hedge onto Shawnee Run for a homerun so many times, going to see if I could spell my Grandpa Luke.

Long and lanky, he had at the uneven green branches with the wood-handled shears, each stroke making a great chopping sound. His white-thatched head bobbed up and down as he moved along the hedge, his elbows thrashing in and out with the strokes.

"Hey," I said. "Let me know when you get tired. I'll get the ladder. Gosh, Luke, it takes me a day to do what you've done already."

"Okay, Bo, boy. You can take a whack at it in a minute. How does she look? Even?"

"Just like Lukie's haircut," I said.

"Swell."

I sat in the grass under a maple tree and watched him.

Over in the side field Dad jockeyed the Gravely tractor through the high volunteer grass and snarled honeysuckle. It ripped and buzzed as it decimated the grass and weeds. At the rate he was going he would finish pretty soon and we could all go in and take a nap. Maybe I could sneak off to Ruth's.

"We should turn Dad's little monster on this hedge," I half-shouted.

"What's that?"

"Nothing," I shouted.

Grandpa Luke stopped chopping, the shears hanging down from his long arms. Then he let them drop. He pulled a bandanna from his hip pocket and swabbed his forehead and stubbled cheeks. His cigaret dripped from his mouth. He stepped back to examine his work. He was breathing hard.

"Take a break," I said. "I'll go up and get Mom and Grandma to make some lemonade. It's too damn hot."

Then I said, sitting under the tree, looking up at him as he stood there, "Why didn't you tell us about being promoted to Judge whatever it is?"

"You heard that, have you? Well, I figured the cat would get out of the bag. But who cares about that? We are here assembled to celebrate a graduation, are we not?"

Turning, he threw himself at the hedge again, his thin arms holding the shears going like crazy.

I was thinking of when my brother and I had visited him in California and he had taken us in to Los Angeles and wanted us to see the La Brea tar pits and kept asking people directions to the "big bones," wanting to ask if he remembered that; instead of that I stood up and said, "Hey. My turn."

He turned to wave me away. Then he stopped using the shears and slowly sat down in the grass right there before the hedge. His knees just folded up, and he was sitting in the grass.

I went to him.

He sat with the points of his bony knees thrust up, rubbing his stomach with one hand while the other held the wood-handled shears. He looked at me with a kind of half smile, as if exasperated or bemused.

"Whew," he said. "I feel a little funny. I'm all right. Had a pain just then. Must be a touch of that indigestion your grandma warned about. Be a good boy and bring me a glass of water, will you, Bo?"

"Sure—You're sure you're all right?"

He nodded. Then he winced and bowed his back, sitting holding his stomach now with both hands.

Clumsily I trotted up the lawn to the house. The sound of the tractor snarling mowing the weeds and high grass continued in the side field.

I met my grandmother as she came out the front door.

"Where—" she said.

"He says he feels funny," I said to her.

She looked down to where he sat.

"Get some hot tea," she said. "Tell your mother to get it quick."

Then she called out "Luke!" and went running down the yard, a small woman with white hair flying, stopping just an instant to kick off her shoes. There had been such a strange look in her eyes.

Mom said nothing, boiled the tea, too horribly composed. I went back outside and around, waving at Dad. He couldn't hear me. Finally he saw me. I pointed to where Remember was bent over Grandpa Luke, who now lay straight out in the grass by the hedge and the maple tree. Dad cut the engine and ran towards them with heavy lurching strides as I also ran towards them and Mom came running out with the mug of tea.

He was wheezing too much to take the tea. Remember said, "Run get a pillow, Bo." She looked like she was made of white marble as she kneeled there. She cradled his head in her lap, as Luke half sat up. "A cold towel, too," she barked.

My mother, her face suddenly become distorted, hurried with me to the house. "You get them," she said. "I'll call the Rangers."

"What is it?" Gramp Tom said. He was standing on the porch.

I ran back out with the wet towel and a pillow, getting them mixed up together, passing my father coming up. "We better call an ambulance," he said.

I knelt by my grandfather and Remember, handing the soggy pillow to her. She placed it under his head, and took the towel and wiped his forehead with it. He closed his eyes, then opened them again.

"Hey, Luke?" I said.

He raised his head and looked at me. He tried to sit up more, but she prevented it. He wasn't wheezing now. He took a sip of tea, then winked a bright blue eye at me.

"What's all the fuss?" he said. "Hey, I wouldn't miss your graduation—Bo, old pal— For the world—"

"Lie back," she said.

But instead he tried to sit up more, then wheezed, gasped for breath, lay back. Mom and Dad were there. I heard the kids, Luke and Joy, run down, heard Dad order them to go back to the house. I don't think they did, though I am not sure. Time hung. Then we heard a siren. The wheezes became wrenches for breath, then hideous rattles in his throat.

His color changed. His eyes shut.

A bright red car crunched into the driveway. Car doors slammed. My father pulled me up and away from him, one arm around me tightly, the other around Mom. He smelled of sweat and dirt and flannel. His old hat was cockeyed on his head. They put the respirator over my grandfather's face. Remember, crouched by him in the grass, looked like a girl. An ambulance pulled in the driveway, and a young man in crisp white knelt by Grandpa Luke with a stethoscope that sparkled in the sun.

In a moment he stood up. They took the respirator thing away.

Luke Whitlock lay long and thin and frail-looking in the grass. The horrible rattling had stopped. His face was faintly blue, but its long lines were soft, relaxed, as if in sleep.

"He's gone," the man said.

My mother gave one sharp sob. Her mother sat like stone.

"No!" I shouted. "He's not!"

My father tried to hold on to me, but, wrenching, I broke away. I stumbled to the stupid man in crackling white standing there with his dangling stethoscope and grabbed his stupid arm and shook him furiously. "Do something!" I said. "Try! You can't go! Goddamn you—"

He broke away from me. My father, like a bear, got me in both his arms, arms around my arms and chest, his hands locked in front, with immense firm strength, himself shaking too, and wrestled me to the ground. I fought him, trying to rip his hands apart, to burst free. I tried one mighty bridge up from the ground; then collapsed. He let go gently and rolled away and lurched back to his feet.

I lay there weeping in the grass.

They put a blanket over my grandfather. It was too short. The men in the red car left. Mom and Dad went up to the house with Luke and Joy. Remember sat by her husband's body. Sitting up, I saw my other grandfather silent as the Sphinx, now sitting again, smoking, on the porch. The ambulance people had Luke on a stretcher now.

Remember got up and adjusted her dress at the waist. She gave a shake of her head, her soft white hair. Looked at me, sitting in the grass where my father had pinned me. Her eyes, blue as Grandpa Luke's, blue as their daughter's, as the sky, were clear and dry.

"Get up," she said. "Stop that. We have things to do. For you. Come on, Bo. Get up."

Without speaking to him we passed my father, coming down to see the ambulance off, and without speaking Remember and I walked up the long front lawn and into the house.

How my mother and Remember, and all of us, got dressed and to the graduation ceremony I do not know.

My teachers Ben Stockwell and Mr. Ash stood there to greet us. "I admire you all very much," Ben said.

"Thank you," my grandmother said, shaking his hand and giving a sharp nod of her head. "This is what we came for."

Tom Northway wore a blue suit and a bright blue necktie. He was immaculately shaved, and silent still, had simply retreated to his room to make his preparations for the outing. Dad held Mom's arm. Joy had been emotional, then recovered. My brother Luke was withdrawn, his eyes hooded deep behind his glasses. Jake Stillman came and embraced me, robed in our Commencement gowns. Ruth was worried about me. We moved to the strains of the Hill school's Alma Mater to our seats up on the stage, then stood together singing "Ye Servants of God." And I felt removed from it, above it, the ceremony then, as if I were in the cartoon of "This Is A Watchbird Watching You": seeing my parents, family and friends in the seats below, looking for Grandpa Luke there, wondering if I would see his long, kind face suddenly above them all, smiling at me, there after all at his old pal's graduation . . . . Absurd, I felt it was. Jake won a senior award, for loyalty, I won one for scholarship.

Afterward, we all went to the reception in the school's formal garden. My buddy Wolf had come to celebrate my graduation. He came and hugged me. He said he had something really incredible lined up down on the Little Miami if I could break away that night and needed some consolation for my loss. I said Ruth would not approve.

"Well, congratulations and lamentations," Wolf said. "I'm sorry, Bo. He was the fisherman not the farmer, right? So you'll have to write about it. Take it easy, Bo. I'll be seeing you, buddy. Don't do anything I wouldn't do."

Home, graduation over, the relatives having called and been called over the nation, the funeral arrangements made, everyone collapsed.

Gramp Tom holed up again in the "memorial" room. My mother and father went to their room, Joy and Luke to theirs.

In my parents' room they were in their robes sitting with pillows behind them side by side on the bed. I saw that he had been emotional but she, so far, had not. The Bible and "The Spiritual Key" sat on the table by the bed. I had changed to casual clothes.

"I suppose you'll be out late," Dad said.

"It's supposed to go to dawn, you know, Mark, with breakfast at Jake's," my mother said.

"I'm not sure I'll make it through," I said.

"Be careful driving," Mom said.

"That might be a good idea, not to stay up all night," he said. "There are things for all of us to do tomorrow. Luke's brothers are coming in, and Aunt Cora . . . . "

It sounded, just then, too much like an order. He looked too vulnerable, sitting with his glasses off, looking so beat. I wanted, in that instant, to hit him.

"We—" he said. Then he said: "Do be careful, son."

From the dining room downstairs I picked up the small package that was Luke and Remember's gift and unwrapped it. From her a volume of Dickens that had come to her from her father, Milo Hathaway. From Grandpa Luke, his ivory-handled fishing knife that I had always coveted, with a penny taped to it. I put the book back on the table, put the knife in my left pants pocket, and from my right pants pocket pulled the old round watch that my Gramp Tom had given me, gold, that General Marcus had given him when he graduated from dental college. And went into the den room, where my grandmother was sitting alone.

"Can I do anything for you?" I said.

She shook her head. "Going off to your party now?"

"I'm not sure I feel like going."

"What do you mean?" Her eyes flashed. "We all went to your graduation. Do you imagine that anything is to be gained by your staying here and moping now?"

"Grandma," I said. "Remember. You do believe, don't you, that he's not gone? That—his spirit is alive, and with us, and—and that he's all right?"

"Yes. Certainly. Luke is right here with us, my dear Beau, and always will be."

"I'm having a hard time making sense of this. Not just that it should happen now—but of death."

"We must think of it as natural, Bo, as setting free from the bondage of the flesh, as freedom evermore from pain, as our wages finally being paid. At least, in my faith."

"How do you have faith?" I said.

"Why," she said with the only irony I had ever heard her use, "a question that confounds my scholar grandson—" Then her marble-like face softened. She smiled at me and her eyes glowed blue fire. "You just decide to have it, my Beau. Now get going to your graduation party."

I got my brother Luke, who had been waiting in his room. He had not changed clothes. He was coming to our party, as usual without a date. We got in the gray Plymouth and headed out.

"I hate him," Luke said on the seat beside me.

"No, you don't," I said, steering along the tree-lined road. We were going to pick up Ruth.

He scratched out a cigaret from the pack in his pocket and lit it with an Ohio Blue Tip, and I could see the thick glasses rimmed inside with tears like rain on a windshield, and his burr-cut hair that stuck up like a half-mowed field on his round head in the flare of the match. I felt one long sob through his long boy's body, then felt him give a quick sideways nod of his head like Northways do.

"No, I don't," he said.

We went in Ruth's driveway and I went to the door for her, and he got in the backseat and rolled the window down so he could smoke.

Old Lady Marlow was graciously letting us use her lighted pool and grounds for our graduation party. There was music and dancing on the tennis court. Ruth wore a cool, starched, backless dress of white. She pressed in close to me, her head going down on my shoulder as we swayed slowly to the rhythm of "The Gypsy." "I'm so sorry," she whispered.

In a while she led me out of the circle of light and people, beyond the pool, removed from the party, to the dark edge of Marlow's woods. We sat on the rough grass that was a little damp, and I remember worrying that her dress would get wet or stained. We sat there for a long time without saying anything. Then she said, "It really is going to be over now, for us, isn't it?"

I was full of several deep and separate pains that came together then. I stood up and left her sitting there and turned into the woods. It was dark in there. A branch lashed at me. I did not go far but stopped and for a moment wrapped my arms around a tree. It must have been a maple, for it was smooth and cool. I heard the phonograph music of the simple songs we had grown up with. I turned back and stepped out into the double light of the strung lights and of a sharp beginning moon. I thought Ruth had left. But I had come out some degrees off from where I went in. She was still there sitting on the grass. I went there and sat back down by her and put my arm around her smooth brown lovely shoulder. She came close to me. Her hand touched my face.

"Oh Bo," she said.

ENTHUSIASM

Then, that summer, my father and I were together "on the road again," this time on quite a long trip in the new little green Ford he'd traded the Plymouth for, a hell of a real trip, in fact, the two of us, all the way to Texas. How we came to embark on this extraordinary hegira, in that lovely summer of '49, the new gold-seekers, requires some recounting.

I was, out of high school and on the way to college, full of ants and romantic ideas of writing, yearning for some grand adventure in this summer of my 18th year. Also I was dodging work. I went down to the Terrace Tavern a couple of afternoons to have a cold, bitter brew with Vince and

Baldy, but I was glad not to be riding the goodies wagon with them. Wolf was out on his own too; he'd found an old man down in the village where he lived who had invented a screwdriver that lit up so you could screw anything day or night, and was busily and happily forming a company to manufacture it and sell it far and wide. A huge black kid called Tar seemed to have replaced both of us at the work of cans and saws. "Young Bo here looks to have become a man of leisure," Vince said.

"I'd say Bo has got so smart on us he don't have to work for a living," Baldy said. "Looks rich as Rockefeller, not a callus on his hands."

"I hear Wolf stole that patent from that old man, and is about to be the rich one," Vince said.

"That there Wolf is the one getting rich, if he can stay out of jail, you ask me," Baldy said.

At Dad's suggestion, strange to say, I was reading Galsworthy, and was in early summer, following graduation and Grandpa Luke's dying down by the hedge, enthralled by "The Apple-Tree, the Singing and the Gold" and devastated by "Indian Summer of a Forsyte," the serene passing of Old Jolyon sitting on the summer lawn. Ruth and I still saw each other in a friendly way; but she had started dating others, including to my amazement some older guy already in graduate school in architecture or something. In my daze I knew my Megan must be waiting for me out there in the world, somewhere . . . .

And Dad was strangely gentle and lenient with me, about not working, as if he knew how I felt, how the ants were marching through and tormenting me. Though he was hard on Luke, who was having trouble with math and Latin and having to go to summer school, which was why I alone got traveling orders. He would have taken both of us if Luke was not such a dimwit, Dad said. Luke glowered at him and said he had no desire to go to Texas. Only fools had ever gone to Texas, Luke said to me.

Ah, but I was wildly excited! It became the focus of my romantic dreams.

Sitting out on the terrace with my mother one sunny late afternoon just before my father announced his plan and commandeered me for the expedition, I sensed her feeling pensive, or apprehensive, or something other than her usual self. She had helped Luke with the Latin. Joy was off on her bike. We were waiting for the Squire to come home and inspect our accomplishments of the day. Mom smoked as we watched the sunlight stipple the branches and blossoms of the apple trees in the side orchard. It was an old orchard. The trees were gnarled now. Worms had come in the small apples that used to be hard and taut but were getting mushy now.

"We sat out here the other evening," she said. "He's been so serious. Things haven't been going any better for him at work. He feels by-passed. That must be a terrible feeling for a man. I tried to get him to relax, to laugh, to plan ahead. You know that is what he most loves to do, make plans, set goals. I wanted him to think about our dream again. You know what it is."

Their dream had always been to have a little place on the water, preferably Florida, and to have a boat, a real classy boat, preferably a motor sailer.

"I suggested we had enough, with this 'chickenfeed'
Aunt Ida did leave us, to look for that place in Florida, to
pay down on it. I went and got our book we've looked at
so often with all the pictures of the boats we talked about all
through the years, the Skipjack, the Bermuda Sloop, the
Cape Cod Catboat, the New Haven Sharpie. And he did
laugh and say that was what they used to call him at Yale.
All the sea-going sailers, and the smaller motor sailers that
we might actually be able to manage. Oh, it would be fun
for all of us, for you and Luke and Joy, too!

"But— He didn't light up to it, Bo. I was serious. I think
we should get after it now, if we are ever really going to."

"What did he say?"

"He said, 'That might not be too good an investment
right now, that Florida land is inflated now.' 'When wasn't
it?' I said. 'And I'm not talking about an investment anyway!'
He had been thinking, he said, that we should use that
inheritance money for 'something good.' And do you know
what that turns out to be?"

I shook my head.

"'I was thinking we might go down to the Valley,' he
says. 'The Valley?' I said. Dear God, Bo, I had no idea what
valley he was talking about, of all the valleys of the earth
and moon. 'The Rio Grande Valley,' he says. Oh, can't you
hear him? 'In Texas. Why, they grow three or four
crops—vegetables, cotton, citrus—a year down there! It's
the new Garden of Eden of the world, Louise!' For thirty
thou, my Bo, we could buy a couple hundred acres. Old
Gerald Elton has checked it all out for him, that's how he
got on to this. 'It would be like having a lien on the mint,'

he said. Then he lit up, talking about going down there and investing what we have in . . . the Valley . . . the new Garden of Eden of the world . . . . And I think he is going to do it. It's his new enthusiasm. And when he got excited about it, his hand—began to shake—really shake . . . . "

"What is that, Mom? Sometimes when I look at him and he's just sitting there, reading or thinking, his face gets all set, rigid, like a mask."

"I don't know," she said. "Nerves, he says. From the will and all that stress, and then my father's—We will have to find out, what it is. Don't you mention it to him!"

And he came home and gave me hell for forgetting to hoe the spuds, and that night I could hear them talking for a long time in their room, and in a week and a half we set out for Texas in the little Ford, ostensibly to visit Gerald Elton.

This Elton was a character. He was 86 and had retired down along the Rio Grande where he had a small citrus farm. The trees had all died in an unusually severe winter his first year there, and he had replanted the entire grove. God knew how long it would take for the new trees to yield fruit. It was the kind of faith and courage my father admired. Before that old Elton had been in and out of our town promoting his ideas and his books, and Dad had befriended him so he was often with us. He had been frozen, when young, in a gold field in Alaska, following some wild adventures in the Australian Outback, and had lain in the hospital in traction, one side paralyzed, for a dozen years. He spent this time developing his theory of Character Analysis through study of the Features. There were Adrenal Motor types and Thyroid Sensory types, like me and Luke, respectively, and very few Nearly Balanced types, of which our father was a glowing example. My mother seemed to escape classification. "Lady Northway" was simply "a Rose." Gramp Tom, old Elton said, was a pronounced Thyroid type, of a rather dangerous extreme. Elton himself, Gramp proclaimed, was a "p-pronounced Quack-a-roony type." But Dad loved Gerald Elton and was intrigued with his theory, as he was with all possible signs of knowing "character," and having it.

We were soon deep into Kentucky, traveling early in the morning, and somewhere between Louisville and Paducah he began to give me lectures. They were lectures because they were so serious in tone and were not discussions, since I had no replies worked up, the greater part of valor on my part being just to listen. He had given us lectures edged with a moral imperative all our lives; sometimes scared us with them. I remember being scared, even at so advanced an age as fifteen, at what seemed from his relating the almost certain prospect of atomic warfare whenever the Russians got the Bomb. We would (though subsequently we never did) dig our shelter and stock it with cans of tomato soup; I had a few lessons in using my .22 rifle, in case the neighbors had no shelter or no soup and came for ours and we had to shoot them. Younger, at twelve, say, I remember resolving to help Dad defend our land when the massed Asian and other Communists of the world came marching up the road across from us to take the Hill. We would meet them at the hedge.

First he told me about geopolitics. I had heard all that before. Then—he had read a book called *The Road to*

Serfdom by "this fellow Hayek"—he went into F.D.R.'s policies of national socialism and the danger to individual freedom of national economic planning under any banner.

"Ben likes Roosevelt," I said, "and he's pretty smart, isn't he? He predicted Truman would beat Dewey."

"Hah!" Dad grinned over at me from behind the wheel. "As it turned out, Boom Boom Beck could have beaten Dewey!" Boom Boom was a journeyman pitcher who'd hooked on with the Reds who threw an "oofus" ball. "Ben is a good guy, and a good teacher. I take it he doesn't indoctrinate you with his own beliefs, but tries to teach you the whole scope of things."

He laughed, I didn't know why, then saw it was at himself. "I'm the one who tries to indoctrinate, I guess, but that's my privilege, being your father. Oh hell, this is pretty heavy stuff, isn't it? I wonder, son, if you even think or worry about these things? You and your friends. Sometimes it drives me nuts, thinking about the future and what it will be like for you guys."

A little later, heading in to Cairo and the river there, he said: "It's just that there seems to be such a change in values. I know F.D.R. tried to help a lot of people who couldn't help themselves. But as a result money and power seem more important in our society than ever before. They were never the real measure of a man. Character— integrity—and ethics were most important, as I understood it. The old order that I learned under seemed to lose standing with Franklin Roosevelt and his ideas and actions. He preached in act, if not in word, that the end justifies the means, that power is greater than truth. That's my opinion

91

of him, anyway. And we ain't much better off than our atheistic enemies if we believe that."

It was the first time I had ever seen the mighty Mississippi.

We sat in the car at an observation point up over the bank. It was twilight. First moonlight was falling on the swell of the great river. A hush, a kind of eloquence of silence, seemed to brood over it on its massive meandering by and beneath us.

"Gosh, it's great," I said, as we beheld it. "Mr. Ash says that rivers are great symbols in our unconscious, in the collective mind of man—"

"In books they are symbols," Dad said. "In life they are part of the great reality of things. They're full of the force of water, and they're wet, and they have strong currents, and they change course, and affect a lot of things and people. Old Mark Twain wrote pretty good about rivers, about this one. I take it you've read him?"

"That was what Mr. Ash meant. In *Huckleberry Finn*—"

"*Life On the Mississippi*, I meant, that's the real book about it, not the made-up stuff." My father's sense of novels was to give enjoyment, his favorite being A. Conan Doyle's *The White Company*, starring the courageous little one-eyed knight Sir Nigel Loring.

I kept on. All my teachers were fairly absolute. It was fascinating to hear one knock another. Meanwhile the great river swelled and coiled out before us from where we had parked to see it.

"Mr. Ash says Mark Twain had a good joke going in *Huck Finn,* how everything was free and natural on the river, and degenerate and sinful up and down it."

"I don't catch the joke, I guess, son."

"That people are—what?—perfectible, and progress is possible, when they're really not."

"Horseshit," my daddy said. "Some joke. If people aren't perfectible, or at least capable of getting better, we'd better turn in our union cards, old Bo."

That was a strange way for him to put it. He disliked unions about as much as he did Roosevelt.

But then we quit the words and sat and looked at it really. To me it was haunting in that moment, isolated from us, remote, as old Mark said, the water ageless, glass smooth at this hour, with the wind died down. It was pale and immense under the first moonlight. It was so incredibly real with the red sun and first white moonlight upon it that it overbore the abstraction of it in my mind. Not gorgeous, not noble or thrilling or glorious, but immense, cold looking as a silvered mirror, even frightening.

"Whatever," I said.

"It's something," my father said.

We cut across that corner of Missouri and holed up in Poplar Bluff late that night in a rundown "tourist court." He didn't want to waste any money on this trip. We'd brought a duffel bag each for baggage, and Mom had packed enough sandwiches and apples and oranges for our first three days on the road.

I lay on my narrow bed, the ants tuned up inside, half-itching on the outside, sure there were bedbugs in my sack. In the dark I heard him chuckling over in his.

"What?" I said.

"Have you heard the joke, son, about the fellow went to court to change his name? His name, see, was Franklin Delano Shit. So he went to court and had it changed to Joe Shit."

I heard him turn over, laughing; then in a while he was asleep, and I lay there and listened to him snoring happily.

Dallas excited Dad. As a traveling man, a salesman of rubber goods for a company out of Akron early in his career he had been here, and had told me of it more than once. It was a golden place to him. He was a Sunbelt guy before they knew the term. He predicted fantastic growth and prosperity for Big D. Dallas' skyline featured a building with a Flying Red Horse atop it. (Now in the incredible glass and steel cluster of the skyscape you can't see that building, that old red horse, anymore.) We motored down Main Street, me driving carefully.

"Some of the best-looking, best-dressed women in the world can be seen at five o'clock at the intersection of Main and Akard, right here at the Adolphus and Baker Hotels, son!" he said.

"Wolf Abrams' brother was stationed here," I said, "at the naval air station. Wolf said his brother said he hardly saw a woman in Texas who didn't have a tattoo."

"Well, I'm sure," my father said "that it's possible to find 'em that way if that's the way you like 'em!"

We drove out into a swanky suburb to say hello to a friend of Dad's. This was a character who had developed a philosophy and a set of books and manuals on super salesmanship. His philosophy was to "sell the sizzle not the steak." You see it around you now in our value-demented society all the time: "Don't sell the contest, sell the spectacle," and other such neo-Romanism. His wife gave us a cup of coffee that sold the pretty cup and not the coffee and the guy and Dad had a talk full of the old pizzazz, kind of like two football coaches comparing bowl games. The guy started in on Dad to move to Texas, to take up one of his franchises for salesmanship training in one of the booming Texas cities, and make a killing. Dad glowed. This was where the future was, all right, he said. I thought, my God, as Mom's sense of his "enthusiasm" dawned on me—he might just do it!

As he stood there in his baggy traveling khakis I saw how vulnerable he was: sidetracked at the station, where now they did the dreadful wrestling and dumb quiz shows (that gave people something for nothing) in the local programming; aching for a new challenge, to take hold of some opportunity of great possibility, especially if it could be to teach, to have an impact, to be wise, to motivate! (And then his strange not understanding when Luke and I both became teachers, and our amazement that he didn't.)

"That guy has hold of one of the great truths of life," he said, driving away.

I wondered out loud what it was. Surely not the "sizzle."

"Well, son, what is the most important quality that you can have in what you do, in your relationships, in your life's

95

work, that you can share with others so it makes a real difference to them?"

"Knowledge?"

"Sure. Granted. But, given that?"

"Intelligence?"

"Well, that wouldn't hurt, of course. But it's not the long suit of us Northways, I'm afraid. We are not especially brains, but we are pluggers. And we tend to overdo things just a bit. We are all like your famous farmer great-grandfather Lige Northway up there in Geauga County, when told plowing six inches would be a good thing, he'd plow a foot!"

"So?"

"Enthusiasm!" my daddy said, inadvertently accelerating. "That's it, Bo, the crucial thing. Enthusiasm! That is really all that fellow has to sell—to be enthusiastic and really believe in what you're selling and that it's doing somebody some good!"

"But you don't really believe in that, his slogan, 'sell the sizzle not the steak,' do you?"

"Why not? Of course I do! It's the greatest sales technique to come down the pike in a long time. The steak has got to be there, of course."

That got him thinking about steak, and hungry for it, and telling me about Gallagher's Steak House in New York, one of his favorite places, where they had photos and clippings of famous ballplayers and racehorses from the past on the walls. He'd taken that damn fool Harry there years ago, and Harry with his dull unimaginative lawyer's mind had bet him they couldn't cook a steak exactly as he liked it, which was charred outside but rarest pink inside, and they'd done it perfectly, and Dad had won a sawbuck off Harry, which, he said, did not even up the later Aunt Ida balance, but helped. So we went to a famous steakhouse restaurant in downtown Dallas, where he had been taken by a client or two in the old days, where they had steaks and roast prime rib. We might as well blow ourselves to one good spread on the trip, my daddy said.

We changed clothes in the car on the parking lot, but our slacks and sports coats were so wrinkled from being stuffed in the duffel bags that I was embarrassed as we entered the fancy, bluelit restaurant with someone playing the piano softly in the background and were seated by a guy Dad said must have just come from a wedding or a funeral. Then I kicked myself for being embarrassed and apprehensive as we sat at the table with gleaming white cloth and silver and crystal and my father, the old sales- man, took his fork and then his knife and spoon and rubbed each carefully with his napkin, as I suppose traveling men did by habit as they ate in joint after joint from place to place, and I sat looking at the menu and praying the service would be good. When it wasn't he also had a habit of getting up and leaving between the salad and entree, even if he'd eaten the salad or a little bread. He had no tolerance for people not doing their jobs well.

I need not have worried. Our waitress was gorgeous, and the service all that could have been desired.

The woman excited me, callow youth that I was. She was a big woman, must have been in her thirties, with green eyes, and amazing smile, "ample bust," and red hair of that deep auburn color of Maureen O'Hara's, whom Dad dearly loved. He really turned on to her, sitting back in his chair at our table like a king and smiling his big rare smile, and really looking handsome for a guy his age with his "Nearly Balanced" features, his intense brown eyes and his noble Roman nose. He remarked on some cliche stuff about Texas that made me cringe, but she responded with high good humor to all his witticisms. He asked her could they cook a steak charred on the outside and red on the inside in this joint and she replied that all cowboys ate their meat that way. (Not true, of course. The cowboys and ranchers I've since known cook their cow till there's not a memory that blood ever flowed in it, as I would do too, in that profession.) He pointed me out to her as his Number One Son, and I managed a little hopeless Chinese grin and she said wasn't I a fine-looking young man with a fine big chest. She had a voice soft and Southern as syrup on flapjacks and was from Tyler, Texas, which she explained was the Rose Capital of the World. Dad asked her what strain of rose was she? It was like that.

When she brought the mammoth steaks and steaming baked potatoes she leaned over me with her smile and green eyes and perfume and breasts just about in her peasant blouse and asked if she could "work my potato." I nearly passed out right there at the table.

The thing was, she adored him. I think she would have followed him out of the place if he'd asked her to, gotten in the car and gone away with him, that is, if he was heading west, to some romantic place. I had seen him so clearly often, from the too-close angle of vision of his son, as a stern authoritarian figure, as a sentimental guy with a hoe among his spuds and corn, and then, lately, as one unsure, his hand shaking, that I was amazed to see this vitality, this obvious attraction to women. When we moved into the lounge of the restaurant after dinner and Dad had a cigar and a glass of brandy and sat down at the keyboard of the piano, Maureen O'Hara followed us in and kind of stood by him, and I could feel her desire to touch him, his magnetism to her, as he began to play.

To me he looked much like that photograph of the old General, Uncle Marcus, whose namesake he was, with that slight Oriental cast to the eyes, that dark black-English flush to the fair features, as he sat there cigar cocked in his mouth, grinning, happy-eyed, finding the first chords on the keyboard.

But what he played then, Sir True Heart, was a simple song he had composed, that began " . . . for I will love you, forever, and ever . . . " and stayed just about there and was his and Mom's song, his ever faithful message of love to my mother. And the vivacious waitress seemed to sense that, and left his side, and went back into the dining room and got back into her waitressing, and just smiled and nodded to us a little later as we left.

As long as we were in Texas, Dad said then, we might as well see some of the fabulous Lone Star state. I heartily agreed.

We drove from Big D down through Waco to Austin. It was about the most boring country I had ever seen, just flat and indiscriminate as to trees, not much geography to it at all. But Austin was pretty, with the hills starting up around it, and we ambled on down to San Antonio and stayed at a hotel right next to the Alamo where they said Teddy Roosevelt recruited the Rough Riders in a dark old bar paneled in dark wood. We sat together in a booth in that bar and Dad ordered us each a beer, something never heard of in Ohio called Pearl, and grinned and clinked his glass to mine. It was the first time we had ever drunk together.

I could not believe the softly shaped mission building next door was the Alamo.

"Why, it's too small," I said.

"I'll bet that's what those old boys inside defending it thought, too," Dad said.

We walked together reverently into the shrine.

It was a few rooms with plaques and dusty flags and cases with dingy glass tops with bits of stuff like knives and rifle balls and odd pieces of clothing in them.

"Look what they fought with, son," Dad said. "The odds were overwhelming. Not a man was left. Jim Bowie, the guy who invented the Bowie knife, see here, fought with his knife from his bed before they tossed him up on bayonets."

"What was he doing in bed?"

"Good question. Maybe he'd had a little too much the night before."

"That was the other guy, you know, Davy Crock-ed."

Dad took the back of my neck between his index finger and thumb and squeezed. His hand sure wasn't shaking then. It hurt.

"My God," I said. "Look here at Crockett's vest and leggings. Why, he was a little guy. This looks like it would fit a kid."

"Yes, well, a lot of these bozos were smaller than we are now, Bo. It was before Wheaties."

Outside in the sun we stood and looked again at the old low piece of building.

"It's a symbol," I said. "It's become one of our great symbols, no matter what really happened there. During the war we sang, 'remember Pearl Harbor as we did the Alamo.'"

My father laughed. It ticked me. I was serious as holy hell.

"You literary chaps are full of symbols, aren't you? Just be careful you don't reduce a real event or person, son, to a symbol. There were real men there—Bowie, Davy Crockett, Travis, whoever else, some Mexican guys too who were for Texas to be independent, I think. Now those names sound like myths to us, like Sir Nigel Loring or Mike Fink or Pecos Bill or Robin Hood, made-up myths that weren't real. But these guys were real men fighting for a cause. You know?"

"Sure. Granted. But what's wrong with taking it as a symbol too?"

Dad pushed his hat back on his head and fished a crumpled pack of Spuds from his britches and lit one of the mentholated cigs. He stood in the Alamo courtyard and thought a minute.

"Nothing, in one sense. The Alamo stands for bravery and holding out for a cause to us now. Just so it ain't taken to mean one bunch, say a white bunch, is better than say a brown bunch, for openers. But I guess what gets me about symbols like this—the Alamo—which isn't just literary so no one but professors really care about it—but is a powerful symbol to all of us, is that it glorifies the damn thing. You know what I mean, Bo? Like the battle, the fighting and killing and dying, are right and—glorious."

"I know it wasn't glorious."

"Oh? You sure? How? You ever had a thousand Mexicans coming at you with bayonets?"

As we turned away, he put his hand on my shoulder. "Did I get moralistic again? Well. We Northways have always been more for the ploughshares side of things, though as you know some of them did go and fight to defend their beliefs and land from time to time. You have my grandfather's journal from the Civil War."

I didn't say anything. I wished everything didn't have to turn into a lecture. I felt robbed of a noble moment standing before the Alamo, reverencing its symbolism.

Dad imitated his father, Tom Northway, stammer and all, as we walked away from history, whatever it was: "'B-but what did they fight them for, she said—'"

We loaded our duffs and duffels into our gallant little pony and made a circuitous route down to the Rio Grande Valley, the veritable Garden of the World, to a little town in a county called Hidalgo where old Gerald Elton lived and had his acres of new orange and lemon trees. This town, too, was called Alamo, which got me to thinking about symbolism again. Alamo sounds so brave and lovely, doesn't it, to have its Spanish meaning be a cottonwood tree.

Air-conditioners in cars were unheard of then, and as we approached Eden it got so horribly hot I thought we had made a 180 degree mistake and were headed straight for Hell. I was more sure of it than Sherman was when he said if he owned Hell and Texas he would rent out Texas and live in Hell. I mentioned this to my jolly father.

"He was an Ohio boy, Sherman," Dad said, "so he was obviously spoiled by our cool Ohio Valley summer climate. He and old 'Useless' Grant planned the war in a hotel right there in Cincy, you know."

We kept driving south, from doubt into desolation. We got a block of ice somewhere and put it in a tub in the front seat. I sat in back so the little stream of melting ice-air would blow on me. "It must be a hundred and twenty," I said.

"I have told you a million times not to exaggerate," my daddy said, unfazed. Some of the fields were green as we reached the upper Valley but most were dead brown, cracked. The orchards looked shriveled. The country was flat as a pancake.

Alamo sat just a short distance from the fabled Rio Grande river. We drove by our instructions to the abode of Gerald Elton.

He had about 200 acres, much of it set, or reset, in what looked like dwarf trees. It was hot and cracked and dusty there. He came walking to us as we got out of the car from his little four-room house. It had alamos around it and was painted white as a New England Puritan church. Old Elton seemed massive from a distance when you weren't sure of the perspective, and plenty big up close, too. His body

resembled the great twisted trunk of an oak, his right side
paralyzed, right arm useless, left leg and foot dragging
across the driveway. On his head was a great shock of
white hair like some separate entity. It kept moving around
on his head inside or outside, whether there was any wind
or not. His craggy face was beautiful—surely he was the
one true Nearly Balanced type—with its big gentle eyes and
its darkened skin like old leather and the forehead lines and
vertical seams and smile crinkles etched by nearly nine
decades of a lonely, suffering life full of romantic adventures and strange ideas. As he walked forward with his
great broken body—he was still straight as a tree, and
nearly six and a half feet high—I felt a deep sense that
approaching us was some part of my father's secret self
made bone and flesh and will. Elton's gold-rimmed glasses
glinted in the sun, his white crown was a-flow, his black
eyebrows bushy.

"Ah, Marcus," he said in a voice like the great Tom clock
of Oxford I would hear years later, "and young Marcus, my
dear friends. Wel-come to my hum-ble a-bode. I am so
glad that you could come."

Inside his house he had an evaporative cooler. It was
pleasant. He had strange Indian and African masks and
brightly woven rugs and antique weapons, a spear, a bow, a
Spanish musket, on the walls. Until we ate at his darkwood
table he stood while we sat and talked, or listened to him.
That was because the getting down and getting up, the
raising of the leg and body, the leaning on the big thorny
cane, took so long. He talked like that—all I could think of
from Mr. Ash's English class was *sonorously*—made

pro-nounce-ments, always. The way he boomed each
syllable out, e-nunci-ated, made my father's lectures sound
like conversation.

Dad sat in a beatup leather chair with brass feet and
studs and beamed at the old man like a boy.

"Well, Marcus—Bo, boy—" Elton said. "Tomorrow we
will go look at the choice piece of prop-er-ty I have found
for you. It is right on—a-bove—the river. Five hundred
acres of the choic-est land. If you are interested."

Dad beamed.

"Bo here thinks it's hot," he said.

"He is a young man of tre-men-dous perspicacity."

I won't try to show how he rumbled "perspicacity."

"Looks like you might need a little rain," I said.

"Ah," he said. "They tell me, it may be a bit soon, yet. It
rained twice in the spring."

"Great," I said, and looked at Dad. He just smiled and
winked at me like the drouth was some wonderful joke
between us.

"It's truck, vegetables, that I'd be raising," he said to old
Elton. "They irrigate for that, don't they?"

"Some do, Marcus. At con-sid-erable expense. I do not
wish to lead you astray. Some years are fine, with rain, and
the river does not rise out of its banks and flood."

"Flood? My God, Gerry, there's not enough water in that
stream to get your tootsies wet. Wetbacks, my eye!"

"Flash floods is what they call them, Marcus. Hardly
unusual. And between flood and drouth, the truck and
cotton farmers have plagues of various her-bi-vores. You
must not think it is a primrose path. I hope I have not

encouraged you to shoot Folly as she gallops. What does the lovely Lady Northway think of this prospect? It would be so good to have you dear ones down here from time to time."

Dad avoided reporting on Lady Northway's predilections.

"Don't worry. Looks like a real sweet investment. You came down here—"

"And got frozen out, Marcus, re-placed all my trees, and do not now know when or if my admirable pigmies will grow or bloom, or if I indeed will see them—"

"That's great, Gerry! Of course you will! You wouldn't have planted 'em if you didn't believe so. Why, hell, you'll be here planting a whole new orchard of 'em when you're one hundred! Do you realize what a guy this is, Bo? What he's done and been through? You'll have to get Gerry to tell you about when he was prospecting in Alaska."

"I'd love to hear it." Again, I thought. I had thrilled to the telling of all that years ago when I truly was a kid; but the ants were eating at me now. The trip, all the sights, the endless miles, the heat, were making me more restless than ever, and a little piqued. Texas was turning out to be all talk.

Then old Elton boomed forth a most as-tound-ing intelligence.

"I have taken the liberty, young Mark, of pro-curing for you a date, cross-eyed and Adrenal-Inclined as you are. She is, I must say, a lovely girl. Her name is Rose. A local maiden, a rare beauty, to my old eye. She is the child of my dear Serafina who helps me here and resides in town, in Alamo. I have assured Serafina, Mrs. Martinez, of your honor and your virtue. She awaits you in—ah—an hour, at dusk, the romantic time of the two lights. That is, if your father can see fit to let you navigate around a strange country on your own in his automobile in the, ah, dark."

I looked at my father. I never would have asked him such a thing. He smiled and nodded. Not even this curveball could wipe that happy prospector's smile off his face.

"Be careful, son," he said, flipping me the keys. "He tries to tell me he's grown," he said, grinning at Gerald Elton towering there above us.

"I have instructions for finding her and squiring her," the old man said. "She will be prepared to be taken to the town picture show, and driven around the town square, and returned home sub-sequently."

"I'm kind of tired—" I said. What does she look like? I wanted to say.

"She is a rose, and a dear, and you will a-dore her," the old boy said, giving me a ponderous Aussie Outback wink. I jumped up to escape the winks. Boy, I didn't have a thing to wear that wasn't wrinkled to a faretheewell. She would think I came right out of the *Grapes of Wrath* . . . .

It didn't matter. She was so pretty and sweet and fresh, that girl, my Rose of the Valley, that I was delirious with joy the whole first part of the evening. Her mother gave me the Eye but was very nice and said not to be late and went out with us to inspect the Ohio plates on the car as if this was a marvel, and told Rose to be sure to do something and be sure not to do something else, as I gathered, in Spanish, and let us go. Rose said she had a bunch of brothers, but praise

God they did not appear. Her laughing mouth had lips that really were like petals, and her dark eyes shone with good humor or mischief or whatever, and her cheeks flushed red when she laughed, and her complexion and skin were like petals too. She was small and wore a dress so white and starched she seemed to glow in the movie theater in the dark. We saw a film a couple of years old called *The Unconquered* with Paulette Goddard and Gary Cooper. When they came over the rapids on the raft she reached and took my hand, stupidly free and not around her shoulders, and clutched it tightly. After the movie we drove around the square, me embarrassed as hell by Rose screaming out to other boys and girls in cars or walking around, and then drove around the town. It looked like a short date.

"If you want to make out a little," she said, "I can show you where to drive."

I shrugged in a manly way, as if it were the least thing on my mind, but followed her directions, steering the little Ford along dark side roads as she cuddled up against me and told me where to go.

"Turn in here," she said.

The road in went through a little arch, and in the head-lights I saw it said Descanso. The place had little groves of trees and lots of white crosses and stones that gloamed in the moonlight. A lot of them had wreaths or real or fake flowers on them.

"It's a cemetery," I said.

"Pull over there, under those trees," she said.

We sat there for a moment with about a thousand ghosts. The little dry leaves from the trees kept dripping on the car roof with a tiny dry, hollow sound. A sliver of new moon hung in the black sky. There were no stars. I'd always thought the stars at night were big and bright in Texas.

"A Turk's moon," I said.

"What's that mean?"

I always thought of a new moon being like a scimitar. "Nothing," I said. I was completely disoriented here, with Rose, in a Mexican graveyard. It was spooky. It did wonders to calm the old libido.

She curled up next to me and put her hand on my face. I flinched, like it was a snake.

"This is a pretty neat place to park, don't you think?" she said.

"How come more cars aren't here?"

"Some of the kids are scared to come in here. It's better than the park though, Bo. That is not very private. My brothers go there with their gang to rock the cars."

I kissed her in gratitude for not taking us there. A kind of moan came from the tombstone off behind us.

"What was that?"

"The wind. Don't you think?"

I noticed she was trembling in my arms and didn't think I was a great enough kisser for that to be the cause of it.

"Are you scared?"

Leaves ponked on the car. Voices of the wind or ghosts hissed sibilants around us.

"Yes. You?"

"Let's get out of here," I said.

"It's just as well," she said as we drove to her house. "I look older, but I'm only fourteen, you know."

"No, I thought you were about my age."

She tapped me on the shoulder, pleased. I thought how lucky I was to escape that cemetery and her sweet young embrace.

"I'm saving myself for Tommy Sanchez," Rose said. "He's in high school and plays football. He's a lot hand-somer than you. He thinks he's a big shot, but I'll catch up with him."

"I have no doubt of it," I said.

She said that she would write, and sign with kisses and with Rosa, which really was her name, and bless her, she did, a nice letter as from a sister saying what was going on in Alamo and that Tommy Sanchez had broken his wrist so maybe she would get to sit with him at the games, signed with lots of XXXXs.

Next day we went to the prospective piece of property, driving in Gerald Elton's big old truck so he could sit up in it. He drove with a specially rigged gearshift so he could work it, and he drove ponderously, right down the mid-stripe of the road. No one honked at him either, they just headed for the shoulder.

It was a flat spread of land, untended now so it looked a little cracked and rough, and brown. But it might look nice all green with crops. There was no house or anything there, just the land. Dad's eyes shone. The heat clouded up his glasses, so he took them off and wiped them for a long time looking at those acres without their benefit, nodding his head, his naked glistening eyes with the marks under them where the glasses went making him once more look so terribly vulnerable.

"God, son," he said, "have you ever seen anything more beautiful?"

We returned home to the hot, humid Ohio Valley, and he bought that land down there a little later in the summer, in time to put in a fall planting. Old Elton was right. Dad never got anything from it but drouth and flood and lies from the guy who farmed it and expense. But still he loved it. Even after he sold it, years later, after I had fulfilled my destiny and Gone To Texas, he was excited that the guy who bought it struck natural gas on it. That confirmed his idea of its value, though his own greatest hope for it always was the crops, the vegetables, the growing things which such land should in abundance yield.

Anyway, not then, or ever, did he let his pennon droop. Like his little one-eyed hero Sir Nigel Loring, also a Quixote of his day, he kept it high for all to see as he faced all that would beset him. I see him, that great heart, my father, as if he were a knight continually going forth to face adversity, to seek fortune, emblazoned, gules and or, on the pennon he raises as he rides, his signature and device: Enthusiasm!

INITIATION

The first time my father visited me at college it was early fall.

The campus, and the way to it in from town, was ablaze with the foliage of fall, red and green, orange and yellow. He came walking in from town the five miles to the campus, leaving his car behind so he could walk in as he had when he was a student there himself 25 years before. He came, he said, just "to see the place again" and, I suppose, incidentally to see me.

As he trudged down the road in, in hat, overcoat, businessman's suit, and bow tie, all the old trees stood firm along the road, Ohio's glory, the oaks and elms and maples.

He stopped to pick up a buckeye. He rubbed it glossy and slipped it into his pocket. He hadn't carried a lucky buckeye in years! About a mile before the college he cut off into the woods by a path he remembered and found the rapidly running little river by which he had so often read and reflected in that time after declaring independence from General Marcus and searching for his own self-definition. He stood still by the stream a moment, then headed back for the road. Off in these same woods was secluded his old fraternity lodge. He entered the gates of the college and passed by the stone cross commemorating the vision and commitment of the Founder and walked down the Middle Path towards where I lived in the big old three-story dormitory at the edge of the campus. It was, though in a different wing, where he had lived in the college.

From my room I saw him stop and stand and look and see what he expected: the old building at the end of the path with its towers rising and the great Bullseye windows set in each tower. Did we still sit in those high, paneled Bullseye rooms, he'd written me, late into the night looking out at stars and talking endlessly of God and Man, the nation and our Selves? I did not know, for as an intimidated Frosh I had yet to venture up there where the known illuminati were said to congregate. At any rate from my window I observed my father, in his overcoat and old brown hat, sit for a moment on a bench by the path, looking towards us. When I ran out of the building he was walking on the path again. Seeing me running to him he lit into a smile. I had trouble not jumping up into his arms like a child, for so far I had been estranged, sad and lonesome in

114

this place that had meant so much to him. Instead my father's hands came out to me, man to man, and I took them both.

"Where's your beanie, Frosh?" he said. "Did your group win the Tug of War?"

On the way up to my room he showed me where his dearest friend Skin McGaw had lived. They had fought each other bloody for some reason when they first met, then washed off in the river; dressed up as badmen from Montana the Dance Weekend; been initiated together in the lodge, given each other the secret grip. Skin knew a thousand songs and made up more. He became a language prof and was killed while serving in Intelligence in the War. A tough little mutt, he had gotten into it even though he was over 40. But, oh, the times they had together!

When I took him to my room we found not only my roommates there but a bunch of other boys from up and down the hall. The college was a true microcosm of humanity, and quite a spectrum of that variety was congregated in my room. It was a small, isolated men's college, and the boys always filtered to where the outsider was, as if to reassure themselves that parents and others still actually did exist in the real world outside the campus.

Tony Laffer was drinking iced gin in a mug lying in his filthy chinos on his bed in the corner. He was skeletally thin, an abusive kid older than the rest of us. I was almost glad he did not speak but thought he might have nodded at my father. He had an old Hudson car whose top was wider than its bottom and would go off in it for days and return to stay drunk for another set of days, almost never going to class. Why or how he stayed in school I did not know. The stink of gin and cigarette smoke hung in his corner of the room; a pile of his dirty clothes lay by his bed.

Bob Peck was my other roomie. He was a bright-eyed, friendly boy from New Jersey. "You're Turk's father?" he said, jumping up and shaking hands. "Holy Smoke. Glad to meet you, sir. Gee Whiz, nice to have you here."

Old Bob Peck said "Gee Whiz" and "Holy Smoke" a lot. He was going to major in physics.

Also in the room were Cannonball, a boy from New York City whose head suggested the name; a boy named Snake who was a wrestler; a tall black guy from Africa who was supposed to be a prince there; a big fat boy who weighed about 300 pounds and would constantly say "pardon me" for stepping on your feet named Dante Carbo; and a chap with an outsize head named Ludwig Neidhardt who was reputed to be the nation's top freshman brain in math. Bob Peck had his shoes off, and the powerful odor of his feet filled the room. How one person's feet could be so pungent was a puzzle to me; I kept a jar of Airwick open on the windowsill near my bunk and never shut that window even in blizzard conditions.

Dad shook hands with all these guys, saying something terribly adult-sounding like "glad to see you men." The husky boy who lived at the end of the hall and never spoke to anyone and was said to be a genius poet poked his head in, looked at us and smiled. Taking an objective camera-eye step back for a moment it occurred to me that I had never seen so many weird guys in one room.

This was Middle Wing. Guys would either stay here or pledge a fraternity and move into the frat wings at either end of the building or into other dorms. Some of the guys were what the frat guys called "spooks" or "birds" who either would never get a bid from a fraternity, or would never want one, guys like Ludwig who was brilliant but looked like Java Man and could care less about socialization on his way to his eventual Nobel Prize, or Bob Peck who opposed fraternities in principle as "undemocratic." "Gee Whiz," old Bob said, "who needs 'em?" Laffer, of course, lonely misfit that he was, scorned us all, Fratmen, GDIs ("Goddamn Independents") or whatever.

There were also a crew of guys like Snake and Stony Van Epps in our wing who were pledging into fraternities. Stony was a pledge to my father's fraternity. He was a neat guy who impressed me with his willpower. He was off now studying in the library. Sometimes he would study all night there, sleeping just an hour or two. I was a legacy to my father's fraternity, but right now I was confused and didn't know what to do. Not that those guys had really approached me yet. "Rush" was so loose and certain, informal and inexorable, in the college that it was like divine election of the Chosen. I suppose you could have been there two or three years before you realized you had been passed over.

I had come to college without my friend Jake Stillman, who had decided to serve in the Marines before college. I was confused because, except for Stony, I hadn't met any fraternity men who were so great. Nor had I begun to penetrate the obvious group of writers who hung together on campus because I was terrified of them. And this bunch of "birds" that hovered up and down our hall in Middle Wing were pretty damn nice guys, I thought, even if weird and hard to take at times, like when Dante stepped on your foot the third time that day. When we had walked the distance into town to the women's college there and were marching around that campus looking for chicks like a bunch of sailors in port, Ludwig would go running into dorms or buildings ahead of us terrifying girls with his looks and his one joke, math-related as it was: "What comes after seventy-five?" If a young woman was brave enough to reply, "Seventy-six," Ludwig would roar at her: "That's the spirit, har har har!" That, and Dante's size, made it hard to demonstrate offhand our attractiveness to these maidens, who, isolated as they were, would surely have been open to the proof; but old Bob Peck and I were soft of heart and could not be rude or cruel enough to leave Dante or Ludwig or Cannonball behind, so we all marched happily along, har har.

Now a bellow came from the doorway as someone passed by in the hall: "Attention in there, you assholes! Bend over and grab your balls!"

Everyone jumped. A few grabbed for their balls. Poor Ludwig almost jumped out the window. Laffer sloshed his gin. Even Dad jumped, and turned to the doorway.

"That's Happy Herm," Snake explained. "He's an older guy, twenty-four or something. He was a Marine, in the Pacific."

"Gee Whiz," Bob Peck said. "I didn't know that."

"So how are your studies going, men?" my father said.

Dead silence. Laffer smiled sarcastically and raised his mug to him. It had the college crest on it. Laffer had stolen it one night from one of the fraternity wings.

"We got this one course, hey, it's called the 'Mystery Course,' only Turk here knows what the hell it's all about," Cannonball finally said. "It's supposed to be Freshman English, right? But it's all about Right Names. Like, if you are walking down the path here, and someone asks you which is the dorm where your son lives, you don't say the name of the dorm, because maybe this moron doesn't know the name of it. So you say it's the big dorm with the twin towers and Bullseye windows on it. You know?"

"Operational definition," my daddy said.

"No wonder Turk is so smart," Cannonball said. He had given me the name "Turk," I suppose because I tried to act so tough and cool when I arrived. All the guys up and down the hall had nicknames, except Ludwig and Dante and the Prince, who didn't need them: Snake and Cannonball and Turk and Stony and Pigeon and Slugger and whatever: emblems of our unformed selves, our lack of purpose and definition at this point in our lives. And truly we went around feeling like we were minor comic characters in some huge Dickens novel we might never get out of. Dad looked a little startled, though, every time Cannonball called me Turk. I just prayed my father would not call me "Bo."

"We got this moron Gil Nash tries to teach this course," Cannonball, whose real name was Maurice, says, "and I don't think he even knows what the hell he's talking about, right? How can we pass this course if we don't even know

119

what he's talking about? This Nash sits cross-legged like a
Buddha with funny little fangs sticking out his mouth, man,
on his desk and says, 'If I sleep on a desk is it a desk or a
bed?' I mean, man, it's a fuckin' desk, right? I mean, Mr.
Turk's Old Man, if you fuck on a fuckin' desk it's still a desk,
right? Jee-zus, what else is it, a fuckin' fuckola? Who cares?
Hey, Prince, man, you come in through that window, is it a
window or a door, hey?"

The Gold Coast boy shrugged. He was having enough
trouble around here just being as big and black as he was
without waltzing in through second-story windows.

"Anybody comes in through that window, we begin to
worry about him," Dante says judiciously.

"Except Laffer," Cannonball says. "He could just float on
up, right?"

Laffer gives us all the finger.

"Well—" Dad says, looking from Laffer to Ludwig to me.
Ludwig has been staring at him with a huge smile since he
came in, like an ecstatic Cro Magnon man, like Dad is an
equation he has fallen in love with, or anyway like he thinks
he must be a nice man.

Dante, who will go on to be a professor of comparative
literatures and outpublish me five to one, says to my father,
"Is that a Phi Beta Kappa key, sir?"

Dad has thrown his hat and overcoat aside and now
stands, hands in pockets, coat open, in a boyish attitude at
the end of the room across from poor Laffer and his stench.
Behind him hangs the college pennant he gave me from
when he was a student here. The key he loves to laugh
about is on a chain across his vest. God, I think, why would

he wear that here? Yet I know it's part of all that he remembers from that time.

"Oh, that's not Phi Beta Kappa. It's Kappa Beta Phi. We made it up when I was here to look just like the other. It was a drinking club I belonged to. It's all a matter of capacity, we used to say." He laughed.

Dante and Ludwig look puzzled, for it is very much, already, the other key that they desire. They do not dig the joke. Cannonball laughs.

"Holy Smoke, it looks just the same," Bob Peck says. "My father has one." His father is a physics prof up there in N. J.

"Have a drink, sport, sir," Laffer slurs from his bed of sloth.

"Thanks. Maybe later," Dad says.

But he does not take a drink during his visit. When he's gone Laffer sneers and says he doubts my father ever belonged to any drinking club. I don't hit him because it seems strange to me, too. My father hardly ever touches alcohol.

"Nice to see you men," he says, and I see he wants to get out of this den of crazies for a while.

"Yes, sir," Peck says.

Ludwig stands up, all Java-head, and smiles wildly at him.

"What comes after seventy-five?" he says after my father, but Dad is already out the door, leaving the question hanging in the air. I follow Dad, leaving Ludwig, disappointed as a dog who's brought you a ball you won't throw, in the room with the others. Behind me I hear Bob Peck say, kindly, "Seventy-six, Ludwig."

"Come on, son," Dad said. "I'll show you the room I had in this joint. It is one of the few singles. It's on this same floor."

Dutifully I followed him over into the west frat wing.

This was the territory of his old fraternity, he said, telling me what I knew. He supposed it was still a pretty good club. He knocked on a door. An alert-eyed, curly-haired, preppy-looking fellow peeped out.

"Hello, I'm Mark Northway. This is my son of the same name. I was in this house, and lived here in this room, a hundred years ago."

"Hi." The fellow seemed real nice. He opened the door and smiled respectfully at Dad. "I'm Jack English," he said.

Oh Lord, I thought. English was well-known as the editor of the campus newspaper and a sub-editor of the literary magazine. He was a senior. He reached out to shake my father's hand. "Welcome back to Alma Mater, Mr. Northway," he said, sounding stiff and literary.

"Brother English," my father said, taking his hand.

Their fingers fumbled for a moment as the fellow realized my father was giving him the fraternity grip. Then they both smiled solemnly and stood there with their fingers entwined, both hands on both hands, in the mystic moment of this secret recognition of their Brotherhood.

It made me feel strange, dumb and awkward, that there was some bond between my father and this kid he'd never seen before that I did not share.

"Come in," English said. He did not shake my hand, but patted me on the shoulder like a puppy. "It's not much, but as they say—"

It was a cubicle, mostly bed and books and a big typewriter. Not a spot of color or a picture. Dad went immediately over to the old, scarred, darkwood built-in desk.

"Look here, Bo," he said.

His finely shaped index finger pointed to his own initials carved there, then to another set of the dozens knifed and scratched on the surface.

"Recognize that name?" he said. I made out R. B. Hayes. "He wasn't the greatest president, but he was one," he said.

"Say," I said. "He stole the election from Tilden, didn't he?"

"You put yours here?" Dad asked Jack English.

"No, sir. They said not to. Nobody's done it, sober, I guess, for a long time. The Dean said I should consider it an historic marker. I don't know if that was because of your initials or President Hayes'."

Dad laughed. He liked a little salt.

"You men will have to join us at table in Hall for dinner tonight," English said, like it was a royal invitation. "We'd be honored to have you dine with us, sir. And—Mark, is it? Sure, I've seen your name on our legacy list."

"Hey ho," I said, to myself.

Half excited, half feeling like a traitor to my buddies the "spooks" and "birds," I sat with Dad up at the head of his fraternity table in the ceiling-beamed, high-windowed dining hall that evening. After dinner a lot of the non-frat

123

guys got up and left their tables, but some stayed and sang the college's songs, and each of the several fraternities in rotation sang its main song, moving around by date of founding at the college. Dad's was first. This was his meat. He'd been songleader back when he was so happy here. Growing up with all Gramp's and our other family songs I had also learned early to sing of "midnight stealing o'er the earth" and of Dad's Brothers "licking their fingers, licking their knives, wiping their hands on tablecloths and leading ungodly lives." Now we sang of the Founder of the college, who'd smoked the ham, dug the well, raised the dough and "spanked the naughty freshmen well" and of "where's ne'er a frown but brings a smile . . . and hope is truth and life is nigh . . . we have yet a little while to linger—You and Youth—and I—in college days . . . . "

After the singing, down in the dormitory lounge, Dad and I had a talk before Jack English, who had a Buick, drove him back into town. It was an earnest talk but (I was grateful) not too earnest. Jack was going in to see a girl he knew. Dad said I had better hit the books. I must pay strict attention to my finances. He and Mom were not exactly made of money right now. And I should always keep to my goal. Maybe I should define it a little more clearly while I was at it. But bless him, in his happiness at being back in the college, he did not even mention the Russians and the wisdom of making Five Year Plans.

He said that he and Mom were thinking of taking a week before long in Florida. He wasn't sure exactly what he was going to do now. Maybe they could hash out some ideas that appealed to them for the future. Gerald Elton had

taken sick with some malady and was confined to bed, all
alone down there as he was. Dad would like to go and see
about him. Luke and Joy were fine, and he believed that
while Luke did not communicate well he was doing better
in his studies. They all looked forward to seeing me
Christmas.

He left. He had not mentioned anything about my
joining his fraternity, so that I felt it really was my choice,
but knew that it would please him deeply if I did join. I
went back to my room. Peck was studying and just nodded
to me. Laffer was gone.

I sat down to read philosophy. It was an ancient
example of "pure philosophy," from Parmenides: "Either
there is or is not; but Judgement declares, as it needs must,
one of these paths to be uncomprehended and utterly
nameless, no true pathway at all, but the other to be and be
real . . . . "

Pathways. Choices. I read the passage to Bob Peck.

"That's 'pure,' all right," he said.

"It's real helpful. Why do paths have to be so absolute,
so either-or?"

"Actually," he said, "in physics—"

"Never mind," I said.

Outside it began to rain. You could see it through the
yellow orb of light from Peck's lamp against the narrow
window. It had become a raw fall night. I was glad Dad
and I were not walking back to town tonight, as we first had
planned, in the rain and darkness.

Jack English and Stony Van Epps and some others from
the fraternity came over soon after that and "hotboxed" me

and I took the pledge pin from them. No one in my wing seemed disturbed, but Cannonball acted strange that night, not upset but just too eager. I had been invited over to a party in the west wing, with, of all things, girls.

"That's great, Turk, man," he said. "Can you introduce me to some of these guys, hey? I mean, I know Stony, he's a great guy, right? So why don't I go over with you guys to the party?"

I felt terrible that I had to tell him that it was just for pledges and actives of that fraternity.

"Oh yeah?" Maurice said. "Sure. What the hell—Just an idea. But if you'll make sure I meet some of these guys— It's one of the best frats, right? Right, Mark?"

Stony came to get me. Laffer was off in his Hudson on one of his secret missions. Peck was in the lab. I felt okay walking out of there with Stony.

He was a bouncy little guy from the Dutch country in Michigan. After he became a minister and teacher he always said these beer busts back at the college had done permanent damage to his kidneys. His friendship was a true gift the college gave me. It started that evening as I put on my new pledge pin and we walked together over to the party of my new Brothers.

It was a good party. There were good guys in the fraternity. Stony and Jack English were fine guys. Stony was studying history. The classifications and divisions among people did not seem to bother him as much as they did me as I read literature, whose glory was the individual. I lamented in my heart for the "spooks" and "birds," good guys too, I seemed to be leaving behind. None of them

really minded, I understood more as time went on, except
Cannonball. He was so eager. He believed that
they—some fraternity—would notice him. He was so full of
life and eager to join in and give of his vitality to others. I
went to talk to Jack English about it, in the room that had
been my father's. I declined a cigaret. Jack smoked in the
manner of Edward R. Murrow. He was sharpening his
image and collecting his wisdom now, as a senior, before he
went out to report the world, or administer, as it turned out,
its reporting. He went straight to New York and later
became head of one of the networks; even now, he was
cool, formal, but a warm person. It was his fraternity
responsibility to be a "big brother" to me. In his room I sat
in a chair whose leather was so old and cracked it may well
have been sat in by my father before me. I watched the
smoke come out of Jack English's nostrils in twin jets, coil
around the paper in his Royal standard, and disappear.

"You're right. 'Passover' will come to have new
meaning for him. He's Jewish."

I did not appreciate such cleverness.

"I know that, Goddamn it," I said.

"Well," he said, "I don't know what the main thing you'll
learn here will be, I mean academically, but I have majored
in Journalism, Political Science and languages and I have
learned distinctions. They hold the world together. I think
the main thing I have learned, Mark, is this: institutions exist
in their forms and for their purposes. Institutions are only
incidentally, even accidently, about people. Certainly not
about individuals. The whole way we define is through
genus."

"And differentia."

"Sure. And the best news story is always the individual bucking the class, the system. And the most inspiring story is the Holy Fool who wants it all to be One. He should be watched, probably hemlocked, crucified. He's damn dangerous, we've found."

He sat and smoked.

"I'm not sure, whatever the truth of all that is, that I want to have my friendships, for three more years here, to be by category."

He shrugged. "That's a choice, Northway. Making choices is by definition—existential or essential—maturity. Right? (As your buddy Cannonball would say.) I would have thought that you had made that choice. I mean, you pledged."

"Because of Stony. My father. You. I'm not sure I thought it through. We Northways are a little slow, in thinking things through—"

"Don't be fatuous, assume the mucker pose, with me. That's your father's trick, he says 'ain't' when he knows better but wants to show what good old farm stock he's from."

But he smiled. "I agree, of course. Who thinks it through? Most of these fine young Midwest, middleclass men here don't. They just come and do it, if they're white and Protestant, or Catholic, vaguely Christian anyway, and not too poor. Do what their fathers do, eh? So good for you. Believe me, I thought about it. Philosophically. No shit, Mark. Did. Almost joined the 'Jolly.' Happy Herm came to me and said, 'You don't want to join a frat, man.

It's all I fought against. Come join the Jolly with me.' 'I thought you fought against the Japs, the Rising Sun,' I said. 'Came at us with bayonets, screaming in the dark,' he said. Almost did it, because I loved old Happy Herm, the Happy Gyrene Warrior. But look at the Jolly, Northway." (The "Jolly" was an Independents' club named after the Founder. There were only about a dozen in it in the whole college.) "What is it? A club mostly of veterans. Right? Right. I mean, it's really no noble big deal, no idealistic alternative to the fraternity, but in actuality a club of older guys who are in this one way malcontents, who know that they could never sit still for the elements of bullshit and hazing in our rather un-Greek notions of 'Brotherhood' in the fraternity."

"Hey," I said.

"Got wound up. But my point well made, I think. And true. Have you met that Pecksniffian literary crowd yet? You think they don't have a club, even though it's not chartered and named? They scorn me because I'm editor of the campus newspaper. Write editorials and objective stories about things that really happen. That's not writing, you know—"

He put out his cigaret and looked at me, his head cocked sideways.

"As a matter of fact, why don't you join the staff of the paper? You say you want to write. You like sports, don't you? I could work you in as sports editor next term. No one around here is worth a damn at recounting sports."

"What would I do?"

"Why, cover our admirable teams. Soccer, lacrosse, hockey, wrestling, fencing. We are too effete for football, baseball, anything you might have heard of, of course."

He was right. I had never seen a match in any of the sports he mentioned.

I left him and pulled Stony out of the library. We walked the long way into town under wonderful stars and sat in the Sunset Club drinking beer until it and our own illogic convinced us for the moment that we probably could not reform the world until we joined it. As we left some tough townie guys came after us, cursing and shoving us around just because we were from the college. They might have really hurt us if Snake and Slugger hadn't come along and seen us and stopped their car and got us, loopy-legged as we were, back home safe to the college.

"Townies and gownies," Stony muttered.

"Yes?"

"'Nother category to consider."

There was almost no social life except for drinking beer with the guys in the fraternity. Dante, Ludwig, Cannonball, Bob and I stopped going places together, though we all stayed friendly. The freshmen gave a dorm dance and invited the freshman girls from the nearby college. I met a nice girl named Jeanie Terrell from Fulton, Missouri, where Churchill gave his "Iron Curtain" speech. We talked about that and then couldn't think of much else to talk about. Girls were curiosities, suddenly, extraneous to the world of that college. I remember I wore a huge, ribbed white sweater to the dance down in the lounge of the dorm. "You look like you weigh 240 in that sweater. Je-zus, Turk!"

Cannonball said. When the girls invited us over to their place for a dance, sweet Jeanie found Bob Peck. She adored him. She sat and listened in rapt attention as he talked to her for hours.

"I didn't mean to steal her from you," Peck said.

"She was hardly mine to steal, Bob. Do you really like her?"

"Oh boy, do I! She's a sweet kid. She's from Fulton, Missouri, where—"

"I know."

"She said she liked you all right, except— She asked me a few things about you."

"What?"

"Where I thought you got that sweater. Why I thought you had to act so tough."

"What did you say?"

"I said, Golly, I guessed you were just insecure with women, you'd only dated one girl all your life. That you really weren't tough at all—"

"Gee Whiz, Peck," I said. "Thanks a lot."

"Well, Criminently, that's what you told me."

"I'm glad you two found each other. But what did you find to talk to her so long about?"

"The quantum leap. You know? About the parallel there must be between the quantum leap in the physical universe and what happens in our brains. It's exciting, Mark! It would be proof, don't you see, of the importance of the human being in the scheme of things. It would be the greatest hopeful thing for man since Darwin!"

"I see." I guess Jeanie dug it, because they got married and she's been digging it ever since. I looked out our window and saw how gorgeous the moon and stars were over the lovely tree-lined campus, all its domes and spires. We spent so much time at the college being in and looking out, I began to feel like old Whitman listening to the 'learn'd astronomer' in a lecture hall and seeing real stars in the sky outside.

Then, as will happen in the luffs of life when you seem to be existing in a crater of the moon, something real happened. A poet came to visit.

I was thinking of going on my own to see, to hear, him, just to have something I might be able to ask or talk about with the "illuminati," the literary figures of whom I was so much in awe who huddled up in the Bullseye late at night. They seemed a prodigious bunch, then, and I still believe they were.

One said he wanted to write a fantasy, a realistic novel and a Western, and has done all that. One said he wanted to write one beautiful book and die young, and he did that. One said he would learn a dozen languages and become a great scholar of literature in various languages, and did so. One looked doomed, had already as an undergraduate published a book, and had his whole career, at 20, behind him. And the husky boy, the young, quiet, massive genius poet, passed through and by them—and all of us—with his mincing but individual and authoritative steps.

My teacher, Gil Nash, decided me by doing me the honor of coming to take me to the poet's reading early that evening. He was a small, snaggle-toothed, tweedy man who often had a half-wit's smile on his sandy face. But he was full-witted, I knew. I'd read his two books, on Dickinson and on Frost, and I knew he dabbled in poetry himself. He came peering into the room, sniffing like a rabbit.

"Great God!" he said. "How do you exist in this foul stench?"

"The source is gone tonight, so it's not half bad," Peck said cheerily. He remained oblivious of the contribution of his own feet to the problem.

"I thought that if you were going to the reading I could give you a lift," Nash said to me.

"Great, sir. This is my roomie, Bob Peck. Professor Nash."

"Ah! Peck! You're in Cranville's class! You wrote that fine paper on what we do when we 'do' history, the 'made' pattern and the 'making' pattern. Best we had on that assignment, Northway here was simple-minded on that one. Are you interested in going to hear this poet?"

"Irish or Welsh, isn't he?" Peck said. "I forget which. Lyric poet. Great stuff."

"You have read him, Peck? You are a young scientist conversant with poetry?"

"Yes, sir. Oh, I mean, some. In school. You know. Holy Cow. About the father fighting darkness, death. Telling him to rage against it. And that great one, Gee Whiz, all the great language—Like 'water praying, and—'"

"'The knock of sailing boats—'"

"And the weather turning around—Neat stuff!"

"Would you like to come along with us, Peck?"

133

"Wish I could, sir. I know it will be great. Have to go to the lab."

"Very well. Come along, Mark. You might don a jacket, if you have one, over those incredibly weathered corduroys."

I donned the tweed jacket with requisite leather elbow patches that my father had taken me to buy and slipped on my dirty white buck shoes and a tie striped in the college colors, and we were off.

"Young polymath there, your roomie," Gil Nash said, lighting up a fag against the various odors and sounds and darknesses of the dorm, which must have seemed to him a jungle of unformed youth. "You better be on your toes or he'll win the Freshman Essay."

We drove in to town and to the women's college in Nash's old Willys Jeepster. It was littered with baby bottles, pop bottles, kids' caps and sweaters, a lute, tennis and soccer balls, and what looked to be the remains of a picnic lunch from several years ago.

"How many children do you have, sir?"

"Whatever made you think to ask?" He chuckled, driving down the frosty road, clouds of smoke around his head, making his eyes squint at me, at the road. "Define: 'having children.' I have given names to five, so far."

"Sons or daughters?"

"Daughters and sons. The oldest, lucky for me and her and my two boys, is a girl. She is fierce at field hockey and lovely at the violin."

"I have a brother and a sister." I almost said, stupidly, "And a father." I did say, "I'm the oldest."

He reached to pat my shoulder. "So was I, my boy. And my father was that very Nash— Ah! You'll be all right. You'll be yourself one day."

"You write poems about your kids, don't you—about all this?"

I meant all the detritus reflecting his family life scattered in the car. I'd read his little book of verses. It was about all the commonplace scrapes and laughs of life. Then I thought, what a dumb thing to say. Maybe he'd think I was putting him down.

But he smiled, that snaggly, half-wit grin. It pleased him.

"Yes. Kid stuff. Learning stuff. Bicycles. Skating on the pond. Like that good essay you wrote on process, Mark, about your father showing you how to use the crosscut saw, what did you say, 'so the saw does the work.' Learning. Teaching. It's my life."

He was from a distinguished family. He had the highest degrees. He loved literature, loved to teach. He was like my teachers Ben and Mr. Ash at the Hill school.

We sat in an auditorium with a crowd of people from the town and the two colleges. I saw some girls and guys and other professors I recognized. A lectern with a microphone attached and two straight chairs sat on the stage, which was bathed in an ugly yellow light.

"Dreadful place for it!" Nash snapped. "The mike will squawk and the acoustics are lousy. Why can't we ever do anything right?" He looked at his watch. He seemed nervous, as if he was responsible for the whole thing, the arrangements and the poet and how it all went. I wondered if as a teacher and a poet he wanted everyone, especially the students there, to love it so that the event would stand in their minds as a Right Name for poetry and the kind of experience that involves stretching your mind and perspective, learning.

"He's late," Nash said. "He's quite a free spirit, as you would imagine. Let us hope they have kept him from the embrace of John Barleycorn."

At last, as the crowd hushed, a tall silvery man who looked like Dad's old boss Bill Schwarzkopf, that ass, and this short, dumpy, potatoey little fellow in a rumpled jacket and baggy pants walked out on the stage. That is, the tall guy walked. The poet rolled.

He sat down heavily, staring at his scuffed brogans, as his silver-haired keeper gave him a long and flowery introduction.

Everyone applauded. Silverhair sat down. The poet had a book in his hands. He struggled up and to the lectern. He stared in apparent wonderment at the microphone. Silverhair rose and came back to adjust it for him.

The poet laughed then, wrenched at the mike, and made contorted faces at it as if he might eat it. He was as ugly as the frog who's secretly the prince despairing of the magic kiss. Then he laughed, more like a giggle, and began to blaspheme in a growl into the microphone.

"Jesus," said Gil Nash.

The funny little potatohead poet wrenched the mike free of its stand, dropped the book of his poems, and peered out into the darkness before him at the audience, stopping his string of half-recognizable curses. There was dead silence as he began to lumber, almost falling a time or two, getting tangled in the cord, like an antic bear around the stage. Then some of the college girls sitting nearest began to titter, and whispers swept the hall. He looked to where he heard the coeds laughing.

"So you laugh at, make sport of, poets, do you?" he bellowed. He had the most incredible voice and accent. His words were thick and seemed drenched in whiskey, whether this was so or not.

"This will not do!" came a female voice in the hall.

"Old Dean Fitzpeter," Nash whispered. I could have sworn I heard him swallow a snort. "Ah, you sweet young cunts—" the poet's voice sang out, now sweet and lyrically. "Ah, how I would love to lay you in a line from here to—"

Nash did snort. I looked at him, totally confused as to a response to what was going on. He shook his head at me. "Jesus," he said, aloud, then quite loud, to whoever cared to hear. "The hook! The hook! For pity's sake, time for the hook!"

The tall silver-haired man seemed to have heard him, or to have reached the same conclusion. He moved slowly and stiffly, in a heavy salt-and-pepper suit, like a British general sorrowfully surrendering; took the arm of the dumpy poet, who looked at him and smiled, seemingly alert as a beaver. Silverhair led him from the stage. They went out like clearing the stage at the end of Hamlet.

Nash took my arm and led me also out through the stunned crowd of undergraduates, teachers and offended cultural leaders of the town. Outside he fired up a cigaret. The sky was bright with stars. Frost rimed the trees and grass. Soon would come the time for greasy Joan to keel the pot.

"Now," my teacher said, inhaling deeply, "I suppose you will join me in a brew? All may not be lost. Embarrassed as old Long John must be, he'll have to do something with him, take him somewhere. Probably Val Joe's. They were going to bring him there afterward, for a spot. You game to see the elephant?"

Driving there Nash did not say much. I expected him to say, "Define: 'poet.'" But he said, "He's had a hard time of it, you know. I suppose he's on this long tour of the provinces to make some money. Life seems to be a terrible struggle for him to live it yet be free to write."

A couple of other English teachers, Mr. Cranville and Dr. Gallini, Bob and Max, were in Val Joe's with some barroom regulars unaffiliated with poetry when we arrived. I felt silly being introduced as a person to the teachers. We sat at a dark table at the back of the place. Nash got two mugs of beer. I sipped at mine. It was flat and lukewarm. It tasted like 3.2 beer. This will never do for him, I thought, as if I were suddenly part of the host activity too. I felt awfully privileged as the only student sitting there listening to Gil and Bob and Max chew over the comic, bitter bone of what had happened, as if I had made it into some upper circle.

Then they came in. Silverhair stood over us and smiled a thin, icy smile. The poet bumped down like a shark nosing in. Silverhair, handsome as old Emerson, sat by him feigning imperturbability, as if it had been the most marvelous poetry reading ever. The poet's eyes, in the odd light from the revolving beer sign over the bluish bar, looked shot with blood. His face now was pale. He sat with a vacant smile on his face, the round rubbery face clasped in his sausage hands, staring at us. When he spoke it was in a normal tone, though in that rich voice whose inflections I will not try to capture.

"I am going to New York City," he said.

All looked at him. "Ah!" said Nash, as if this was news indeed.

"Yes. New York City. Hah!

"There is a fellow there I'm going to see. This fellow is in Advertising. He says there is worlds of money in it. That's what I'm after now, the money. The fellow says there's thousands to be made in it, in Advertising. Is that true or isn't it?"

He looked, much like a brooding baby bull, at those around the table. None of the English profs seemed to wish to confirm or deny the potential of Advertising.

"You should talk to my father," I heard my voice saying. "He's in advertising, that whole line of things. He had this wealthy old great-uncle who wanted to send him to medical school or law school, but he chose to go into that. Advertising, sales . . . "

"And has got rich at it?"

"No." I felt embarrassed, having to admit it; but I wished Dad was here to talk to him.

"I am not sure that it would be a service to the world for you to turn your talent to the writing of simple-minded advertisements for automobiles and cigarets," Silverhair said.

"The world?" he screamed. "The bloody fooking world?"

He glared at Silverhair, who for the first time looked angry, put upon and pissed off, staring coldly back at him. "You don't think I could do it, eh, write the bloody Advertising?"

"I am sure you could. Surely."

"Surely? Hah!"

He broke into a curse.

"You think that's not the job for a poet, do you? Where— do you imagine—you withered shanks of scholars, you critics, is the poet's place? It's in the world, damn you! Where you could never be—"

Quickly Nash asked him some question about American poetry he did not answer. Instead he addressed the age- and hops-blackened table with continued truculence: "Vultures! Scavengers! Tame the poet in your classrooms. Bloody bunch of bloodless brains—Vipers, vultures, mor-tic-ians—"

Someone had brought a pitcher of beer. The poet slopped a little in his glass, in his mouth.

"I have whiskey at my house," Silverhair said.

"Ah! Shall we go there then?" said our friend, beaming at him.

Silverhair, and Bob and Max, led him off. Nash said he had to get me, and himself, home. But after they left he stayed still.

"Do you think he's right?" I said. "About teachers?"

"In a way. We do take the love and terror of a poem, its truth about the short moment of life and the absurd fact of death and, yes, we do tame it in the classroom. When we do poorly we peg it out on the board like a butterfly, make it wingless. Passion becomes metrics, the whole just parts, metaphors just tricks, equivalences. And, sure, the best of us can handle five poems in a period. But usually, I hope, we don't do that. I wish this one could know with what joy and emotion we discover and are startled by, re-discover and react to his language! Perhaps he does. Yes, I am sure he does. Like here just now. He plays on and counts on our love when he plays us for such bums—"

"Why do you think he wants to act like that?"

Gil Nash shrugged.

"Have you met other poets?"

"Yes. My teacher, Mr. Ash, took us to Columbus once to hear Robert Frost."

"And?"

"He made me think of my Gramp."

"Aha. Very wise and noble?"

"Well. I mean, more like an old farmer. But a real character, like Gramp. We went to a reception afterwards in somebody's house, a whole bunch of kids and teachers, and sat around on the floor waiting for him to appear, and it turned out he had been back in the kitchen of this big house cooking eggs. Then he came in and sat down and talked to us and spoke some of his poems to us. One kid asked him if the less-traveled road that made all the difference was being a poet and he just smiled and spoke the poem again."

"Of course."

"He had a great voice. Like it was all—truth."

"Yes. He's a great poet, the greatest of our time. There is a wonderful voice, in the poems, mark you, Mark.

141

Whether it's all 'truth' won't bother you as you travel on down the road. The delight is in the language, the lines. Anyway, he made a very different impression on you than this fellow tonight, I take it. Well, he, America's favorite kind, good, true, avuncular old prophet of Nature and aphorist in verse played his role for you. How much of the real person do you think you saw? And how about this fellow tonight? How much of him did we behold tonight? More of his insecurities than the other fellow's, I'll grant. But we saw him as in his role as Peck's—not your Peck's—or Poetry's—Bad Boy. Why he does it I don't know, but we can bet he's not just what we saw, a clown, a sot, a boor. So much beauty, grace, intelligence and courage are in the poems. And, of course, for either, whatever the persona, the masks they wear to live from day to day—as we all do, Mark—the poetry they create makes the persona—oh, interesting, I suppose, but irrelevant. We bless them and forgive them everything for the great gift of the poetry."

He started up the car. The lecture hung in the air.

"But you're a poet. You don't wear a mask."

"Oh ho. 'Yes, I write verses now and then.' And pose as a befuddled middle-aged teacher and family man. But the real me within, Northway, is a raging maelstrom of constant inner flighting, a driven madman just barely restrained— Say, how about a proper nightcap after our adventure? You can stay away from the Stygian den long enough for a cup of cocoa, can't you?"

"That would be nice," I said.

We drove to his house. It was a white wooden house of New England design in a grove of trees. His wife was a tall

blond woman who wore glasses and was pretty. She was
reading in front of a cheery fire of apple and black locust
logs. She got up and pecked at her husband, she was taller
than him, and went and made us cocoa. He went into his
children's bedrooms and kissed them all goodnight. We sat
in front of the fire and drank the cocoa. I don't remember
what we said, or saying anything. What I did was fall asleep
on the couch where I was sitting. Then I felt Nash lay me
out and put a pillow under my head, and I knew the couch
was going to be a bed. "Sleep tight, Mr. Marcus Northway,
whoever you may be," I heard him say. "Sweet dreams."
Then I felt his wife bend over me. Her hair smelled smoky
and she smelled cocoaly and motherly, and she put a
blanket over me and tucked me in, as if I were their child.

I went down the hall to the room of the person
everybody said was going to be a great poet. He was a big
kid all kind of drawn up into himself but a nice guy. We
had talked a couple of times and he had been tolerant of my
presence and to my questions. He had told me he was
going to take a year off from college just to read all year and
I thought that was the most amazing thing I had ever heard.
Like most students my age, I felt I was supposed to get on
through and get out and get with it, whatever it was. Now I
halfway wanted to try to write poetry, but I was scared to. It
seemed a mystery, and poets more a mystery. He was in his
room. It was late afternoon. He was just sitting there like a
Buddha with no expression on his face. For a moment I
thought maybe he was drunk or something, he turned his
head around to me so slowly.

"Are you working on your persona?" I said.

He yawned, and stood up and stretched.

"Fucking A," he said. "Let's take a walk."

We walked out to Middle Path, then turned off it and went down the hill and towards the woods and the river that ran there. It was chilly. We breathed deep. The air was sharp in the nostrils but not cold enough to make smoke from your breath. It was November, but a strange Indian Summer time, a small separate season, had come and just departed. Whenever he walked inside, down our hallway or in classroom buildings or to the dining hall, he took small careful steps for such a big person, like a trained circus elephant. Going along outdoors he lumbered. We went along a path in the woods. We sat down on a stump and on a rock near the river that ran sweetly along there, all in flux as Heraclitus said, giving the illusion of unity and continuity, as it had for Dad in his day here.

Right across the river was an edge of field, a meadow with the dark green light of approaching evening on it, and beyond that a little orchard of wild apple trees. An old smoky-colored horse stood between the river and the trees just breathing in and out and munching something real or in his imagination.

"Dobbin," the large boy said, giving the old horse a name or a name to old horses or whatever he was doing. "I like old horses."

"My father used to sit here, right here, I bet."

"And he's still sitting here? He's a big figure in your life?"

"Isn't yours?"

"But small. Quiet, tough and small. All the nobilities I know seem small and tough to me."

A little later he said, "Look at the dark green of the meadow."

"Are you from Ohio?"

"Sure."

"What part?"

"The dirty part. We did have the river though, the 'beautiful the beautiful the river.'"

"I live near the river, too."

"I bet you live above it, tho'. Right?"

"I guess so. Way above, and away, fifteen miles from it."

"I lived on it, growing up."

"You can be Huck, then."

That made him laugh, just for a second, and cut his eyes at me. His eyes kind of simmered in his big, nice face when he looked at you.

"You writing anything?" he said.

"No," I lied.

"Good luck with it," he said.

He got up and lumbered off. I sat in the growing darkness with a little nest of stars forming overhead feeling awfully much alone.

But as it got darker I began to like the feeling; then as it got really dark realized something true and terrible.

As for that large, kind boy, he died untimely and was the finest poet of my age.

We were initiated at the end of that first term. I received a wire from home wishing me luck, which startled me. There was to be the whole long initiation day and night and then a formal dinner the next day with wine and fraternity dignitaries and such.

We'd had some snow that had come and stayed, lying white on hills and layering trees in woods. Now, in early January, it was more likely to sleet and sheet with ice. It was a cold, creaky, windy, dingy time. Initiation day came with just a smudge of dirty orange sun in a cold pewter sky.

There were seven of us in the pledge class. It was a small college; there were only 30 in the whole fraternity. Stony Van Epps was captain of pledges. He was very serious and diligent about it. We had not been hazed much, in terms of paddles and eating dogshit and putting your head in the toilet and such fun and games known to all red-blooded American college frats. We had been run ragged running booze to the initiates and otherwise waiting on them. The only bad times had been when the five or six war veterans showed up to bedevil us. They were scary. They were what we would call "cool" now and any one of them could have starred in his own video. They were dispassionate, cynical, cruel, careless of their own well-being and that of others, and I think really crazy. When we saw them they were always drunk out of their minds but horribly composed and controlled. They were always going to tattoo the Greek letters of the fraternity over our hearts but always put it off "until initiation." They could think of the most exquisitely sadistic things for us pledges to say and do to demean ourselves. Later I wondered how these guys fit into society at all, though they were also Dean's List students in the college, most of them Phi Betes. Checking, I found that all but one became lawyers and then served as prosecutors and judges in major cities. The other became a rabid evangelist on radio and TV and is still at it, right-wing and rich, distorting Jesus.

The coolest and craziest of the vets were Mo Mo Allen and Albert Blue. Mo Mo wore chinos and sneakers with no socks, even in the ice and snow. Albert Blue was Bat Masterson. He wore pin-striped suits with vest and a fedora. Mo Mo had hounddog brown eyes that looked like they were about to crack and dissolve and could never quite focus on you. Albert Blue's eyes were like ice chips. They fastened on you like magnets to your bones and being. The fraternity put those two in charge of us that day.

It wasn't too bad. Mostly we stood at attention in the lounge. They left us there alone most of the morning. Every once in a while Albert Blue or Mo Mo would come in carrying a big paddle and ask one or another of us what we were lower than. "Whaleshit at the bottom of the ocean, sir," was the standard reply. Or squidshit, octopusshit, sharkshit, anything marine seemed to suit them. Albert did make Bill DePrimo assume the position and whacked him a couple times on the rear with the paddle because he said duckshit on the ocean floor and Albert considered that a fallacy. The only bad thing was how drunk Mo Mo and Albert Blue were when we were so absolutely scared and sober.

In the afternoon Jack English and Brother Omega, the president, came in wearing robes like jurists and quizzed us on all the history and lore of the fraternity and had us recite where all the chapters were. Then for about three hours we did push-ups on the filthy floor of the lounge so I got so tired I thought I'd die. For dinner we got some kind of horrible hash all glopped together in a bowl. Then they took us each to a separate room and blindfolded us. I stood there blindfolded for what seemed forever. Then someone came and helped me put my jacket and cap and muffler and gloves on and led me out of the dorm and marched me down the path, then onto another path and then through the woods because the trees were cracking with ice and the branches twinging with wind and then along some gravel and then sat me down on something cold.

"Stay here. Don't move. Keep your blindfold on." The voice belonged to Jack English. "We'll be back for you," he said.

It was cold. I stood up. I could tell I was on the railroad tracks that ran along the ridge above the woods. After a while I took off the blindfold. The trestle was about half a mile off. I could tell because some yellow lights shone there. I started walking down that way. I thought if I didn't move I might freeze to death. I don't think I cared much just then whether I was initiated into all the glories of the fraternity or not.

A figure was huddled up on the tracks on the trestle. It wore a red Watch cap.

"Stony?" I said.

He stood up. "God," he said. "It's colder than—"

"Duckshit," I said.

"Where'd you come from?"

"Down the line."

"I hope the night express to Chicago doesn't come roaring along here. It'd be a good jump off this trestle."

"You could feel it coming ten miles away through the rails. What do you think the point of this is?"

148

"Make us be alone," Stony said. "Contemplate our worth alone in the dark."

"That only took me about five minutes."

"You'd better get back to your place. Remember, Albert Blue said—"

"He's crazy."

"Nevertheless. We have to make it through the Eleusinian Mysteries without a hitch."

"Oh, this is like Jesus on the mountain?"

"Well, sport, that's something else again."

"Boy, I hope so."

"Get out of here, Mark," Stony said, "so we can make it through together. No need to screw up now." He slipped his blindfold back on and sat down on the railroad track again as exemplar to me.

I trudged back to the general vicinity of where I had been left. I stayed standing but slipped my blindfold on. The night was black and starless so it was about the same.

Pretty soon I heard steps. That was good because I was thinking the rails had begun to vibrate.

"What are you doing standing there, Northway?" Albert Blue said. "Jacking off?"

"No, sir. I tried, but my dick froze."

He laughed. Then he led me down the track and collected Stony. Then he took us by each arm and led us down a path. His hands on our arms were strong. His steps were regular, not like he was drunk. He wasn't wearing any gloves or an overcoat. He had been a captain in the Army and fought in battles we had heard of. "You boys be on your best behavior," he said. "This is it. We're going to the lodge."

Then it all happened fast, or so it seemed, even though we had to wait in a circle in silence, blindfolded, outside the lodge for a while, and then as they took us in one by one with a period of like five minutes. We could tell we were all there standing near each other in the cold night and then that they were taking us in one by one. I think Stony went in first. I know that I was nearly last, or really it seemed I must be last.

I remember being led into the lodge. The blindfold was removed. I saw a blur of faces through the flickering light of candles. It was just as cold in there. Jack English stepped forward. Then I saw my father's face in the eerie circle of faces in the candlelight. He was looking at me. Looking at me he looked somehow sorrowful. It was so strange, unreal. It was like we were all shades in some kind of Hades. It was like I was Hamlet and my father was the Ghost of my father; but I could not reach over some barrier, some terrible chasm, to touch him.

Then they put us through the rite of initiation.

When Jack English came around to me in the circle I instinctively tried to shake hands with him normally.

"No," he said.

He took my hand and fumbled me through a novel interlocking of the fingers that was the grip. Then we did it again so he could be sure I knew it. Then my father came forward and I found myself shaking my father's hand, gripping my father's hand in this new awkward way of misplaced, contorted fingers. It was so strange. Then he merged back in with Jack and all the other old initiates and I stood with Stony and the new initiates while they did one last last formal rite of sealing the bonds of Brotherhood. Then we all gave each other the grip again, and my father shook my hand again and I wanted so badly for my father's hands to reach out to me really, like I was his son, I was Bo and he was my daddy; but now we were Brothers, in the ritual something more and something else than son and father, and we shook hands formally giving each other the grip again, and he barely smiled but still looked sad, and stern, and it was strange. Then they lit torches and we all marched back to the dorm together singing the fraternity songs. I marched beside my father.

"Surprised?" he said.

"What?"

"That I'm here."

"Oh. No. I'm glad."

Later that night, as he went back to his room in the inn off campus, all of us who had been through it crashed. I should have been able to sleep but for a long time I could not. Whatever I had been through that night, whatever had been gained, something had been lost. But when I finally fell asleep I felt calm, more adult than boy, a long way from the few months ago when my father had first come to visit here. He was just a mile away and my roommates were in the room but it seemed as if I were alone. I lay for a long time aware of the stink of Tony Laffer's gin and the slur of his snoring and the sweet clear breathing of Bob Peck and the slight night odor of his feet. Now I would move over into the fraternity wing, and room with Stony.

In the Spring term I tried to write poetry for an old lyric poet who venerated the Egyptian Books of the Dead. Unfortunately for our rapport I was under the influence of unadulterated Walt Whitman and the old poet hated my stuff. He advised me to stick to prose if I wanted to write. If that was my aim in life, he said wisely, insufferably, watery blue eyes in brick red face, then "never, Mr. Northway, write anything that is not beautiful and will not last two hundred years."

"Oh boy," I said, to myself.

That summer I realized that I had learned things at that college and was a person different from the boy who had gone there but that it was Dad's place and really not my own. Much as I loved Stony, Maurice, Bob Peck and my teacher Gil Nash, I must now go my own direction.

"DO NOT GO GENTLE . . . "

My father's weakening (though never of the spirit) occurred in stages for a decade after that. I did not see him steadily for several years as he sold the home place of my growing up, moved to another city and took up with all possible enthusiasm a new venture there. Following my own romantic heart and with real readiness after my bleak first college year, I went to Texas and found my place there, and the mother of my children, and a life and a career; but, as they say, that is another story.

I told him of my intention not to go back to the college but to head on down to Texas and see if they had schools there one day as we were hoeing hills of potatoes on our Ohio place the summer after that first college year.

He stopped hoeing for a moment and looked at me. "Why yes," he said. "That sounds good, son. If I were you that is exactly what I would do."

Then he regripped the long old hoe that had come from the generational family place up north in Geauga County where Tom Northway farmed in earnest and began to chop and mound again. As he hoed his hand did not shake though it had begun to shake whenever he was idle, much to his disgust. Mom was insisting he go in for a definitive diagnosis. He was hanging on at the station in his minor position but was restless. He must have put four of our acres under cultivation to corn, beans, berries, potatoes, tomatoes and grapes that year.

"You can check on the Alamo land," he said. Gerald Elton had died at 87, before his new grove matured, and Dad did not trust the cranky German who was farming his land for him. The "Garden of Eden" had been prey to drouth and flood, had one year been declared a "disaster area." So far the investment was a flop. "And you might just as well take the little Ford we went down there in. It's a good time now for you to have your own car. You'd have to be a roadrunner not to have a car in Texas."

"Hey—"

"That's okay. You help people when they need it, right? All my father, your beloved Gramp, who I grant is a character now but who used to be a tyrant, ever gave me was a kick in the seat of the pants and a lecture on oral hygiene. I'm happy to be able to do it. It's a good little buggy. Just keep the oil changed and don't ride the clutch. And remember, you can get there just as fast on the highway if you abide by the speed limit. The smart guy don't speed. And pay attention, you just sliced through that hill. Those little hills, son, are where the spuds live. Have you told your mother of this plan to go to Texas?"

"No. I thought she might not be too happy."

He stopped and leaned on the long hoe handle, looking up at the burnished summer sky. "Yes. She'd like to have you nearer. We both may be upsetting her," he said.

He liked it that I was going to Texas, going to El Dorado, going west to find Cibola, going to school out there on the recent frontier. And that day in the potato field I sensed in him his own yearning for new adventure, for some accomplishment he could put his stamp on. How often in those days he said he was "tired of working for the other guy."

As we kept hoeing side by side going down the rows in rhythm he said, "Did I ever tell you, Bo, about the time Uncle Marcus took me to visit his dear friend Luther Burbank at Sebastopol? This hoeing and chopping here reminds me of it. It was the summer of 1921, I am sure of that, because it was the same time the old boy was seriously trying to take over my life and shape me into his scheme of things, make me his namesake and heir. He'd made me leave State and go off to Yale. So that summer we were at the General's place in San Diego, there in California, and we drove over to Mr. Burbank's 'proving ground' in Uncle Marcus' Packard runabout. Now that was a neat car! I remember the fires burning there, son, where the little guy

155

was burning the rejected trees and shrubs and plants that had not 'improved themselves.' He was a tough little guy, Burbank, in a loose shirt and slouch hat. We walked over acres and acres with him, him carrying big pruning shears.

"I only remember one thing he actually said. He raised his head like he was going to say something real wise—he'd known Emerson, I think—his hair was white and wispy on his head—and said, 'The redwing blackbird is late this year.' He had flowers, fruits, vegetables—Shasta daisies, lilies, nuts, prunes, tomatoes, potatoes, spineless cactus, in long rows. Some said he was a crackpot creating 'monstrosities' but Uncle Marcus believed that his friend was doing it for the benefit of mankind, in tune with Nature, unlocking her secrets, 'improving the dietary of the race,' making the deserts bloom and the world better. Old General Marcus was a little bit of a mystic himself, you know, a homeopathic on the way to Indian medicine man. And those two were a pair in it. Old Burbank called all this stuff his 'new creations.' The General was friends also with Edison—they fished off a dock together down there in Fort Myers, Florida—and with old Henry Ford and Firestone and all that new industrial bunch, and along the way had been a chief medical officer to T.R. in the Spanish-American fiasco. All these guys were 'new creations' too, weren't they—what they were doing in reshaping the world? You should write a book about that, son!"

Then he said, almost sadly: "But he—Uncle Marcus—didn't seem to understand, about advertising, the great new moving force in our society, when I tried to tell

156

him that summer of my interest in it, of my own plans for myself."

"No," he said as we walked back hot and tired from the field to the toolshed to rack our hoes, trailing them by the handles behind us, his hand on my sweat-soaked shoulder fluttering like a bird's wing, "that is exactly what I would do, go to Texas."

My brother Luke and sister Joy made the traumatic move with our parents to the Southern city they located in. Years later after taking his advanced degree Luke went back up to our old country, to teach, and we went off together for a few days to talk and say good-bye. He said he thought our father was not only motivated but driven in a way that made him almost crazy, that much of what he wanted in life slipped by him because he was always looking beyond it. That he kept our mother too much on a pedestal, before she had to come down abruptly from it and work in the vine-yard beside him, then care for him . . . . I register this as Luke's opinion. I had always seen our father, doubtless, as part quixotic knight, courtly, charging windmills, if that is crazy, as if it was just idealism that couldn't quite temper down to life.

Luke told me how it was with Dad after he resigned from the station and was looking for what to do next. In his old brown hat, brown suit and bow tie he'd go to inter-views, but nothing pleased him. To keep some money coming in he sold paint and supplies, as he had sold coffee pots and brassware during the Depression, for a couple of months. Then he took the best opportunity he saw, and put his money on it. ("Remember, son, the smart man picks his

157

horse, pays his money, and rides in one direction.") Clearly
he did not rip up roots and go off on a whim. He went
because he had to. He could not stagnate where he was.

He bought a franchise for a method of salesmanship
training from the super salesman we'd stopped to talk to in
Dallas on the Texas trip. He would have gone to Texas
himself, he told me, but the guy was already there. So he
went to a booming Southern city, though one provincial
and retarded in terms of "tested selling techniques." I think
he was never unhappy with his decision. He made as much
as was humanly possible of new place and opportunity,
pushing himself always beyond what came to be the limits
of his physical capacity.

It was our mother who paid the toll of that decision.

"He had already bought the franchise, made the
decision, when he told her," Luke said. "He informed her.
They were sitting out there on the side patio looking out
over the place they loved. They'd never lived anywhere but
Ohio. All their friends and family were there. He had some
disease that made him shake and slowed him down that
they'd just diagnosed—and he tells her he's bought this
franchise and they're moving down to some city she's only
heard of. There was this look of horror on her face. She
just sat there. Then, Jesus, Broth', in a minute she looks at
him and smiles big as she can and says, 'Oh, wonderful!'"

Meanwhile, I had gone to Texas, to the city Dad loved,
and to the university there. After graduation I married a girl
from Louisiana and became a Teaching Fellow in my
university, trying to make sense of grammar and syntax to
prairie freshmen, taking a Master's degree in English. For

this folly I received the following epistolary encouragement from my father:

"You know what I always say about riding your horse in one direction. Idealistic and sometimes impractical as you are, it is a satisfaction to me that you have consistently pointed in one direction. I wish you would give some consideration along the way to the growing field of advertising, but I am proud of your teaching and overall growth. Your great-grandfather Northway taught country school at 17 and was good at arithmetic, something that got lost in the rest of us along the way. Then there was your great-uncle Jake Northway, otherwise a useless person who trained carrier pigeons in the First World War. I think you have heard that story. Teaching is one of the highest of professions, even with its dullness, routine and niggardly pay. You will learn much from doing it I am sure—whether you stay in it or not."

I stayed at it through the academic year, and after that we went to live for a while in Paxton, my wife's small town in Louisiana, as I began a novel and began to send out stories. The novel was called *Salad Days* and was about that strange freshman year at my father's college. That fall my old buddy Wolf Abrams came blasting through Paxton on his way west and stayed the night with us. He was on the run from a woman who thought he'd said he'd marry her. Wolf had sold the Night-Screw franchise and was on the way to L.A. to take up sales for an anti-bed-wetting device that, when the poor child offended and the wet hit the grid, lit up all the lights in the bedroom and activated a blaring recording of "The Star Spangled Banner." Old Wolf admitted this experience might lead to other problems for the kid but opined he would never wet the bed again. Later I heard from Jake Stillman that Wolf had moved to Nevada, where he was selling slightly radioactive rocks from some acres of rocks he'd bought wholesale for their curative powers. Just unwrap the Healer Rock and put it in the bathtub with you and feel it get to work on your afflicted part.

Then, after Christmas, when I had been free-lancing for six months and sold nothing, and we were broke and had a baby, I agreed with my wife Frances that maybe I should make a move back towards responsibility. Dad suggested the same to me, by phone. It was too late to hook on with the university as a teacher for the spring. I was at a loss. "Why don't you try advertising?" my sly father said. I realized how pleased he'd be if I did.

So I charged a suit I could not pay for, a brown all season number he would have called "a nice set of weeds," and took the bus back west to Cibola, the golden city on the prairie.

There I began a "real life adventure" with one of the great characters, and teachers, I have ever known, an advertising wizard by the name of Gus Baum.

Gus Baum already was a legend, having worked in the city for years before realizing his goal to have his own advertising agency. Now it was one of the largest in the city and the most mobile and creative, for he was known to hire and fire more people in a month than all the other agencies in a year. One story I heard about this large and great man, which I believed to be apocryphal until I saw him, was that he had been so large that one year he lost one hundred pounds and was terribly sad when no one noticed it. My informant in this matter was a fellow from Alabama called Woody, who was Gus Baum's production manager in the agency. I met Woody at a party at the old fraternity house.

"Send in your résumé. Ask for an appointment," Woody said. "Who knows? You might have to wait a while, but he'll probably see you."

Which was why I found myself, as in some absurd existential play, sitting outside the great advertising mogul's door, sitting by his secretary, who periodically, she sweetly assured me, sent back in to him my résumé. I sat there for four days, even after the time Woody said I should probably give it up. Every so often I would behold the great man heave by into his office or surge back out, making everything and everyone tremble as he walked by. He always nodded to me politely, as if I were some misplaced person whose presence there puzzled him. But he had warm, sparkling eyes and a kind expression on his face as he swept by, and perched on his black and silver mane was a brown Dobbs hat just like that of my father, Mark Northway.

The fourth day, after a lunchtime I had not honored, I was startled out of my reverie of being a penniless father forced to take some onerous real job outside of teaching or the golden world of advertising by the voice of Mr. Baum's motherly secretary: "Mr. Baum says he will see you now."

I looked at her quite dazed.

"Hurry up. I think he's leaving town," she said.

I entered the sanctum of the great man. He sat in a huge blackleather chair behind a huge desk. Sunlight streamed in

161

through the windows of the building set in the midst of all the other, mostly higher, buildings of the city whose myth and hype Gus Baum had helped create. His soft brown eyes were hooded with thick, black-rimmed glasses whose lenses magnified them just short of the size of those of Dr. T. J. Eckleburg. His generous mouth had a half smile, his shaggy head cocked as if he heard the song of a lark off somewhere. He looked, again, puzzled, as if he wondered why I had wandered in. His enormous hand rested, as if about to use it, on his telephone, completely hiding it. For a moment I thought the sweet old secretary was playing a joke on me.

But then he smiled a dazzling, embracing smile, the tufts of his eyebrows lifting, and hunched over his desk towards me as I stood awkwardly on his carpet.

"Sit down," he said. "What is it that you want?"

"Thank you, sir." I remained standing, hoping that would make me appear a bit larger, older. "A job. Mark Northway, sir. Woody Brandon suggested . . . I think you have my résumé there."

He looked at the stack on his desk, messing his huge hand through a stack of stuff. He found something that might have been my résumé and creaked back in his great black chair, lit a cigaret and took it down to ash in two puffs. His memory or vision must have blurred on my name, for he looked back up at me and said kindly, "Do sit down, Morris. No sense standing there with a daisy in your ass."

"No, sir." In the guise of "Morris" I sat.

162

"What do you think you can do?" he said, lighting another cig and peering at me like a tremendous benevolent monarch frog.

I took a deepdown breath, reaching for my father's timbre, or hoping at least that my voice would not crack.

"Well, sir, Mr. Baum," I said, "I have been a Teaching Fellow, teaching freshman English, in the university here, and I'm a writer, I mean, sir, I have been writing some stories and trying to get them published, fiction I mean, and my father is in advertising, well, really sales training now, and he thought . . . I mean . . . I don't really have much experience, Mr. Baum, but I was an honors English major and I have always been told that a good liberal education prepares you to do well at anything."

He smiled at me hugely. "Like hell," he said.

And he swivelled away from me, lit yet another cigaret, pawed up the telephone and kind of whistling and looking out the sunny windows began to dial it. With the immense perspicacity we Northways possess, doubtless because of our liberal educations, I sensed that the interview was over.

I tiptoed out. Outside in the anteroom Mrs. Leatherwool, the secretary, clucked her tongue. "Was it that bad?" she said.

I told her and asked her what I should do now.

"Oh, sit down," she said. "I bet he hires you. He liked the idea that you had taught. He walked out of his little Texas town right after grade school, and walked all the way here, but he loves the idea of education, teaching. He's a genius, you understand, but he feels the lack, I think. Just hold tight. You don't have anything else to do, do you?"

A little later he emerged. He went sailing by, then stopped, turned, and regarded me. "Ah, Morris," he said. "How nice of you to wait. Go pack your bag, my boy. Meet me at the terminal at—" He looked at the big gold watch on his massive wrist. "—five-thirty. We are going West."

"Yes, sir," I said. He was already down the hall. He moved fast for a big man.

I called my wife in Louisiana and said I thought I had a job, brushed the suit, packed a volume of Robert Frost and presented myself at the train station. We shared a roomette on the train. I tried to follow him into it but found he took up all the space. Graciously he came back out and I went in and nestled in the upper berth, where I stayed as we rolled on to Abilene and points west visiting Gus Baum's clients in clothing, jewelry and candy stores, and I began to learn.

He liked to introduce me to them in this way: "This is our new boy in Research, Morris. Maybe he will become a Writer for us. Morris Northway. I don't know when he changed his name."

I don't know if he was serious or joking, but he always smiled and put his arm around me when he said it.

One of those nights, in Albuquerque, under the New Mexico moon with the purple mountains surrounding us, we discussed the poetry of Frost, and of advertising. I told him something of my father and his choice in life. "Yes," he said. "Your father is right. Advertising, pure conceptful selling that benefits the people, that gets the products to them so they are aware, is the engine in our world that keeps the steam in the sails of progress!"

Back home, he started me in his wondrous world slowly, as a father might give his uncertain son easy tasks to do around the house. After letting me just carry his bags and drive his car—he had a little car weighted on the right so that when he got in the driver's side it would come plumb—and do twobit research, he put me in the copywriters' bullpen. There I sat among the real Writers, waiting for my inning like a short reliever just up from the minors. The copy chief was a bright young woman as stable as the March Hare. "I am nutty as a fruitcake," she assured me when we met. Every half hour she would pop in on us as we sat before our typewriters in our cubicles and yell encouragingly, "Okay, gang! Let's squirrel those bears!"

My steady bear to squirrel was writing ad copy for a drug store chain called Skillerns, which sponsored the Freddy Martin show on radio. I also got to put together the Freddy Martin show. The trick, for we were scalawags in the copy room, was to see how many terrible Freddy Martin tunes you could program into one fifteen minute segment. There was such a wealth of the soupy songs to choose from that it was a challenge.

I worked hard on the radio spots that ran between the Freddy Martin numbers of Top Tune time. Worked hard but I must admit with tongue heavily in cheek; for I could not really come to believe that this world and what I found myself doing in it were real. Vide this effort:

"This Springtime Skillerns would love to help you rejuvenate your lawn and grounds and take care of all your garden needs. Skillerns is featuring the finest fertilizers at reduced Spring prices—To keep your yard looking jaunty

165

through the approaching hot, monotonous months Skillerns is offering a complete selection of sprinklers, swaying sprinklers, whirling sprinklers—So shop the specialized, super-value, Springtime Skillerns store nearest you!"

"Oh, alliterate me, baby!" the copy chief said. "Oh sweet assonance, oh consonance! Oh shit, Northway. Not only does the client hate it, but the disc jockey says it's impossible for him to read it on the air. Also the client says you are playing 'The Old Lamplighter' too much. 'The Old Lamplighter' is not the client's favorite Freddy."

Mr. Baum called me in.

"Morris," he said to me gently, "the client wants a nice, sharp little piece, to sell what he has got on special in the store. The client wants a nice, sharp roadster. Now I do not wish to be a burden to you in re: your God-given creativity, my boy, but you come rumbling down the road at him with a Mack truck of verbiage that can't get out of low gear, all camouflaged *language,* for God's sake, you hardly name the *products.* This is not college, Morris. These radio spots you are supposed to write represent something *real,* okay? They are not Homecoming floats. Read this over that you wrote." He handed me the piece I quoted. "Who is supposed to be saying this? It sounds like T.S. Eliot when he has been dead a while."

Oh my, I thought, knowing the justice of the rebuke.

"It was all about springtime," I offered.

He looked at me sadly. Shook his great good head.

"Well," I said, trying to carry it off with a bit of bravura, "'April is the cruelest month.'"

"I know," he said. "We don't need a poet to tell us that."

166

I told Dad about it over the phone.

"The guy's right," he said. "It's serious business, son. It's business, anyway. You don't want to clown around. I'd like to meet him. Sounds like I'd like the guy."

The next time I was called out of the bullpen into his office Gus was sitting there with another large fellow, a client who had a line of beverages to push. This fellow had come up with two new wine drinks in cans that he had named "Quicktail" and "Hottail." On the spot they invited me to come up with a ten second commercial.

I stood and stared at them. The client stared at me. The boss gazed out his beloved windows. Loving candy, he had recently bought a candy company and was terribly concerned about a chocolate thief in the candy plant in Chicago.

Over the wall of silence I blurted: *"Beer weary? Try Quicktail!"*

"Thank you, Morris," Gus said. "You may go back to whatever it was that you were doing."

Later I said: "I'm sorry, sir. It was the names."

He snorted, laughing. "Yes. He should have let you name them. You would have done it real poetic, I am sure. It wasn't bad. Just, not good. Now Billy Blaubach, your neighbor who sleeps all day at his typewriter but then is *quick,* or LuAnne, they could come up quick. You are like me, the train is nearly by when I wake up and realize it's on the track. Me, I control the agenda, to compensate. You, maybe we should give you something slower, so you can think about it, have time to be sure you are in the ballpark and also all around it."

So he set me to an "academic" task, writing a long, well researched brochure whose purpose was to attract light industry to a new "industrial district" he was fronting for. It was thousands of acres west of the city of what had been a major ranch in North Texas. In years past it had been famous for quarter horse racing. Generous as always, Mr. Baum said I could also get some experience helping with the p.r. for the big event of the transfer of the land. All the big boys were to gather at the site to close the deal and, with much ceremony and press coverage, a check for millions of dollars was to change hands.

We drove out to the site together a week before the event.

"That old man, the owner, still lives over there, he and his foreman," Gus told me, pointing to a house on the flat land. "One of the famous names, most famous ranches in Texas. We will make up a big, outsize check, and I can see the look on that old man's face. He will be sad to take the check for seven million dollars, to lose this land, and I will be sad along with him."

"Then why are you handling it, if it makes you sad?"

"Huh? Dear God, my boy, I do not wish to be a burden to your fine mind with this philosophy, but this is valuable, idle land. This is the land where the industry will come to help take our city into another age, a whole new period of development. No one cares anymore if quarter horses race. It is time, for everyone, to get into this age and build a real damn city on this prairie. The sadness of one old man, while I share it for all it means that the past is over, such human sadness does not count."

168

"So," he said, "we will have a candy-striped refreshment tent here, and there a platform, and striped tents for the press and media, and— What else do you suggest?"

"Dad always said, when in doubt have balloons."

"Yes!" he said. "That is what we will have. A million or more balloons, Morris, my dear boy, balloons of all colors—orange, red, blue and yellow—all the colors of Texas, of this great southwest where we are so privileged to live in this endless opportunity!"

It was some months later that I visited my family in the Southern city they had moved to. They were living ("temporarily," as they always said then, "until we can get our feet on this funny red clay they have here") in a big, rambling old house on the main street downtown, using it for home and office. It was late fall, which was lovely there, with all the rich colors in the trees as well as the beauty of all the tall green pines. Joy had come to Texas and was a freshman in the university I had graduated from. My brother Luke had been in and out of several colleges and was now out. He was, bless him, hanging in there with Mom and Dad, going nuts, trying to help them, working nights, just being there with them in this unfocused time in this new place they were trying to learn and understand before he made his own move.

Dad met me at the airport in the Gray Lady, the Dodge he'd bought when I took the little Ford. It had push button gears and glided along so smoothly that it was a pleasure for him to drive.

"This little Dodge is a better car than any Cadillac ever built," he said. "It almost comes up to the Auburn I had when I married your mother."

"How are you?" I said.

"Well, I am awfully damn tired of this shaking. It's getting on my nerves. I think I'll go to a specialist. Business so far is bad. We've gotten a couple of big accounts right up to the trough but no deal. These people down here are so unsophisticated they have hardly even heard of sales training and counseling. I'm a little bushed right now. Your grandmother Remember and her sister Lucy were here for a week, you know. It kind of crowded up the joint. They finally caught the Southern back to California. Lucy is eighty, she regaled us with stories of their youth in the country. She's hard of hearing and repeated the stories until we were in a coma. Also she has constantly repeating bowels."

"How's Remember?"

"Feisty as ever. Every night she'd get up to turn the heat up, which is a terrible waste of money around here, and I would get up to turn it down, then she'd get up and turn it right back up. I'm glad you're here to see what we're doing firsthand. Your mother has become a first-rate secretary and office manager. We're working hard to try to turn this thing around, get over the initial hump. For now we've had to take on a couple of extra lines."

Already he was antsy, wanting to shed the franchise and have it be his own operation, his idea, to have his own outfit with branches in Charlotte, Birmingham and Jacksonville.

"So how's your job?" he said. "Still having fun?"

"Oh, I'm squirreling bears. Like I told you, I'm doing research and writing for projects now. Actually, I'm learning an awful lot about the city, and about Texas. Mr. Baum really is a genius, I think. He's a prophetic voice, a big planner, like you. Those two cities are just thirty miles apart but they've always feuded like hell, but Gus sees the whole area, the whole region as an entity, as one economic and marketing area. That's what we're pitching in all these projects. That, and the fact that you've got this great pool of skilled, independent, strong yeoman non-union workers there."

"Smart guy," Dad said. "Sounds good. Sounds like you're in a good position. Make yourself indispensable to the guy, that's the trick."

I did not disagree, did not say how far from indispensable I was, or how grateful for Gus Baum's kindness in teaching me some new balance between romanticism and realism and in just keeping me around to assist him in minor ways. I was happy at this crucial point that I could give my father a sense of security about me, a sense that I was okay and was doing something he understood and considered worthwhile. I imagined it must be a little like when he went to Yale for the General.

My parents' home and office was an old wooden house that used to be grand. It had fine front pillars but the paint was flaking off. It was in what now was a rundown section of the city.

"Welcome to Tara," my mother said, a glint in her blue eyes. Everything was to be positive if not wonderful. She

171

told me they were looking at wooded lots in a lovely newer section of the city.

Luke hovered over us like the Watchbird. "Mr. Christian," he greeted me, in one of the many modes and moods he assumed with which to front reality, slumping, lip out, hands clasped behind his back, "did you steal my coconuts?"

"You're just in time for the Vitamite session," Dad said. "We've got two or three of these product-selling classes going. Come on in, swell the crowd. I told Luke to be Mr. Hathaway today."

I took a seat in the round parlor-like room Dad used for seminars. Four people besides Luke and my mother and myself sat on the straight chairs in the room. Dad stood for a moment by a blackboard on an easel at the front of the room, his shoulders slumped. Then he breathed in, straightened up and seemed to take on several inches of height. He smiled and addressed the group in a Vitamitey welcome, and told them of the efficacy of the food supplement and how much might be made from being part of the pyramid of its sellers.

"You can do it!" he said. "Repeat after me the key ingredient of Vitamite or anything else you try to sell! 'Boy, am I enthusiastic!'"

The response from the frumpy older woman and two seedy men was less than inspiring. My mother chirped her enthusiasm. My brother and I did not manage to rally to the cry. The other gent, an older man of great height and gaunt face dressed all piebald in shiny black pants and white jacket and blue shirt and green necktie with black-and-white two-toned shoes, boomed out his enthusiasm louder than my father's. Dad called on him for testimony. He rose and declared he was a preacher of the gospel of Christ Jesus and a family man and a doer of good works and now a prideful purveyor of this new natural-vitamin miracle food supplement to the populace. While on the one hand he was proud of this high responsibility, he was on the other hand humble in this sense of the blessing he was bringing to the mass of jaded people so in need of Vitamite. Dad thanked him about three times before the rackety old fool sat down. Then, eyes aglow, Dad called on Mr. Whitlock.

Mr. Whitlock, in the guise of my brother Luke, sat in the far back of the room under the impression he was Mr. Hathaway. Looking at him back there, tall and filled out so his length and posture reminded me as I looked of our grandfather, I guess that looking at him sitting there had put Dad in mind of Luke Whitlock.

"Mr. Whitlock, don't you have a testimonial for us about Vitamite? Mr. Whitlock?"

Mr. Whitlock coiled in his chair and hooded his eyes at him.

"He's Mr. Hathaway," my mother whispered fiercely towards the front of the room.

"What?" Dad said.

Mr. Hathaway might of course have lurched to his feet and become Mr. Whitlock and presented a cheery word for the taking and selling of the new green wonder cake; often enough he was Dr. Johnson or Captain Bligh or Larsen E. Whipsnade in our presence; but Luke was in agony over the whole charade and sat in silence.

173

"Well," said Dad, the showman, voice up and richly timbred, "never mind, whoever you are. You are obviously the one in a thousand that Vitamite has no effect on."

But at dinner he said, "Sorry, son. I didn't mean to embarrass you. I'll be glad when we can get rid of these damn sidelines."

That night I went to sleep reading the sales training manual he was writing, which he would adapt to various clients from securities to fertilizer salesmen. It was my daddy, all right.

Selling is not a 'racket' or a game. It is a skilled art that requires the same attention as practicing medicine or law, music or writing. (So there, Uncle Marcus!) *You are dealing with the human brain, human nature and human types.* ("In-dis-putably true," said old Gerald Elton in my ear.)

One of the priceless ingredients of selling is enthusiasm.

How do you generate enthusiasm? No one can give it to you. It cannot be bought. It does not come in pills or bottles. The truth is, you have to generate your own—out of your knowledge and conviction that what you are doing is necessary and helpful. . . .

He had articulated his spark, his "sizzle." He had come tiredly into the room that afternoon and turned it on and become taller, vibrant in eyes, in voice and in every motion. Yet the part of me that was a teacher wondered if this was something you could teach. Could Babe Ruth have taught, to some earnest rookie without his heart and reflexes, his home-run stroke?

The next morning I went with him on several calls to prospective clients. He told me that the warden of the big prison there had asked him to put on a program of sales training for prisoners who were about to be released.

"For free, of course." He laughed. "Some of them are pretty tough cookies. But I think it's a good thing, it probably won't set them back. I do it every Saturday afternoon. I get tired by that time of the week but what the hell. It's kind of nice. Those guys never walk out on you."

His grip tightened on my arm as we walked along together.

"Actually," he said, "who knows? Maybe it is giving those guys some hope."

When we went in to see the prospective clients he would be beaming, his hand outthrust, and the hand would be on the edge of tremor, and one foot lightly dragging.

He went on then for three more years, with good success. He got some institutional accounts, took on an associate and incorporated as Mark Northway and Associates. He and Mom kept the office downtown and moved to a new house among the pines in a pleasant suburb. We all had good times with them there. My daughter remembers my father's humor and vitality from those times when as a little girl she visited them even though one summer her goldfish died and floated to the top of the bowl.

After two wondrous years with Gus Baum, and with great affection remaining between us, I returned to my university in the city there to teach and to assist its president in planning and public relations.

Those late Fifties years were a hard and dangerous time for a university dedicated to the free search for truth and to free, responsible expression; as well as a divisive time for a city too often still tuned to a frontier anti-intellectualism and fear of different ideas. We stood against Know-Nothings delirious about speakers of various viewpoints on our campus or about books in the library; oracles of God decrying the human dignity of the races learning together; a rabble in mink attacking freedom of inquiry and expression; even the Klan rearing its ugly hooded head. But the leader of our university was true as *veritas,* and we did stand through those times. (Not divining then what times of assassination, social chaos, international folly and terror would follow—all calling for the kind of perspective through time and faith in reason which the university offers society.) Inside our walls, we had battles for a curriculum that might bring perspective's truth to students facing this world which was so quickly shaking old innocences and illusions. So that, as we headed on towards Nixon-Kennedy, and the fractured times that were to follow, I had done some battle and felt myself a boy, a neophyte, no more.

That was an irony, for I would be filled with what can only be a boy's feelings for a father's fall.

It was then, approaching the new decade of the Sixties, that my father determined to chance the operation against the dreadful thing that was driving him crazy and countering his drive to accomplishment, the damnable Parkinson's disease.

There was a family conference. The decision was strictly his, though my mother agreed. It was she who explained the operation to us.

She said he had spent so much time in a specialist's office having tests and tests that they'd lost several months' business. It frustrated him. Then the neurologist told him that if he were his age and in the same condition he would have the experimental ultra-sonic operation that a doctor was doing up in Iowa. The alternative was the supposedly more dangerous New York operation done with balloons and alcohol injections, much publicized because of Margaret Bourke-White. My father had comparatively small involvement at that time but a prognosis of it becoming steadily worse. He was in his fifties, and the Iowa operation could not be done in a patient over 60. First they cut out a piece of skull above the ear, then let that heal for a month. Then they shot the sound ray to the affected part of the brain. They'd had good success so far with this technique in stopping the shaking, rigidity and paralysis of Parkinson's.

Dad said the odds looked good to him. My mother prayed that it was the medical miracle they needed. "If it will only give him a few more years when he can happily work hard at what he loves without this physical and psychological handicap," she said.

"My God, son," he said. "I'm going to beat this thing! I'm rolling now. It'll be expensive, but we'll sell some stock and then I can make plenty of money when I'm in good shape again. They make precise measurements, it's all real scientific, so there's not much danger to it, as I understand it. We just have to know it *will* be successful! I sure don't look forward to the prospect of having a hole in my head, but it's a hell of a lot better than this slow crumbling into a shambling old man. Business is pretty good now—and if I could just be more aggressive!

"I want to set up independent consultants in three or four other cities with here as headquarters—teach 'em the business, then advise 'em—for a percentage of the take. Why, it would be like having a lien on the mint! And it's a damn good possibility, if I can just shake the shakes! Look at that circus of birds in the yard!"

We were sitting looking at the birds around Mom's feeder in their back yard, scores of many-colored birds gobbling away.

"We had a nice cardinal couple last year," he said, "but they didn't come back."

They went just before Christmas that year up to the university hospital in Iowa for what Dad called his "overhaul for the next twenty-five years." They went by train. Dad had a private room. Mom stayed in a rooming house a mile away and walked to him each day. They took the piece of skull, above the hairline, out, to be preserved and replaced after the ultra-sound second phase. They stayed five weeks recovering.

He was cheerful. "If one of you guys has a pair of dice, we could get up a game of craps," he would say to the doctors as they trooped in and out surveying him. They returned home and waited another month, and in February went back for the sonic treatment. It was not successful. It seemed to accelerate instead of retard the progress of the disease. In the summer they went back to have the ultrasound treatment again, and I went up to be with them and to take some of the burden off my mother.

Even coming from Texas I thought it was very hot there in the Athens of middle America. One or the other or both of us sat with my father all the time, awaiting and then recovering from the operation. The side of his head was sunken in with the skin flap over it where the skullduggery had occurred. His eyes were strangely moist. They seemed gray instead of brown and were purple-socketed. Mostly he just stared. Some flowers sat in the room and cheer cards were stuck in the venetian blinds. I tried to read or talk to him.

One morning as we sat there, Dad sitting up in bed pretending to be reading something, I with my book in the plastic chair by the grimy window, a minister came into the room. He was for all the world as knobby and unctuous as Uriah Heep. He offered me a greeting and us both some platitudes and Dad tried to smile at him, but then, looking at how pitiful Dad looked the damn fool minister began to weep. I stood up. I would have hit him if he had not scuttled out of there. Then I wanted to cry too, and to attack the famous doctor, the son of a bitch, as he came by to check the result of what he'd done to my father. It was as deep and irrational a feeling as when Grandpa Luke had died and I had attacked the man in white who pronounced it so and my powerful father had wrestled me to the ground.

But later, as we sat again alone—another rare time, for Mom was almost always there—Dad said: "Don't be sore, son. I'm not. It's not the doc's fault. It was clearly labeled 'experimental.' We knew that. It was my choice."

A few minutes later he said: "The only thing I feel sometimes . . . Oh, mostly not . . . I've had a hell of a good life, all the love and good times we've all shared. But I wonder sometimes if I should have followed the old boy's advice. Uncle Marcus, I mean. He meant well. He was trying to put me on a road of power and privilege, through Yale and wanting me to be a lawyer or doctor, not that I was ever bright enough in science to be a doc. I would've, anyway, probably been like this guy here who can't get this damn operation down right, experimenting and screwing people up. Like Burbank. But the old General— He himself was a poor boy who grew up on a farm raising hops up there outside Utica, and he'd found the road, and I know he loved me and wanted me to follow in his steps along that way.

"Well, that thought just comes to me now and then. You know damn well that I've been for the most part happy along the way. Hell, it's been *my* way, the Northway way, which was never the easy way. I guess my real regret is I wanted so damn much to be able—Oh my dear son, it's just that sometimes . . . these past few years . . . it's been so *hard* . . . ."

I remember, as I fled that room that evening in Iowa and went out of the hospital, seeing the only happy people in the whole place playing volleyball in a courtyard. They were yelling happily, surrounded by a mesh fence. They were the hospital's psychopaths. I went and sat on a bench along the path. I looked at the man sitting smoking next to

180

me on the bench and saw he had no nose. Gauze covered up the hole where it should be. The smoke came out of the bandaged hole as from a cave.

The terrible thing then was that my mother, her eyes becoming vague, began to give a little laugh at things that were not funny. She oiled, powdered, rubbed him incessantly as if that could make some difference. I insisted—demanded—she come out to dinner with me for some bourbon and cornfed Iowa beef. I was afraid she was slipping off away from the dreadful reality.

"I couldn't possibly eat a thing," she said.

But at the cheerful restaurant we had some drinks and both devoured our steaks and then had a brandy and sat and talked. She smoked her unfiltered Chesterfields and I bought a Dutch Masters cigar and relaxed and listened to my mother, enjoying the slow smoking of it.

I asked her if it would have been better for him, for them, to take old General Marcus' lead.

"What an odd question," she said. "There's still a lot you don't know, isn't there? My God, Bo, *no!* For many reasons, my professor son."

"Why? You disliked the General all that much? I thought . . . "

"Oh, it wasn't that. Let me give you my perspective, okay? Let me count the ways. Let's see."

She proceeded to give me her perspective on Uncle Marcus Northway, the great physician and surgeon general, the millionaire, the looming figure in the tapestry of our family.

181

"First time, Bo, I saw him," she said, lighting up and taking a deep pull, "was in the summer of 1930 when he and Aunt Ida came through Cleveland where we all lived then and the old couple had both families to dinner at a country club that your Gramp Tom and Mattie belonged to, if you can imagine Gramp as a country clubber. Now Uncle Marcus was born in 1848—he lived to be eighty-six, you know—so he was eighty-two then, and just as spry and sprightly and old-timey gallant as he could be. Aunt Ida, that great tank of an Irish woman, if you can believe this, got me aside to tell me how lucky I was to have married a Northway—'her' Marcus could still satisfy her completely."

My mother paused a moment. Her eyes went almost to gray as she thought, in counterpoint, to the terrible irony that had now come to her and 'her' Marcus.

"Oh well! I was just twenty-four, and your father on the verge of thirty. Anyway, I remember dancing with Uncle Marcus then at the country club, he in his blue coat, white pants and white shoes, and how forceful he was, giving all the orders, keeping conversation going—though later it was Aunt Ida who gave the orders.

"The next year, or year and a half—now it is 1932, the banks not yet closed, your father still with his ad agency, but the Depression in full swing—My mother and Dad had lost their lovely home to unpaid taxes and were living in the old country place of the Hathaways outside Cleveland with Grandma Ada (who lived to be one hundred and three) and Aunt Cora and Uncle Morris (their home gone too), with no electricity or plumbing and outside well water. And Tom Northway had lost all his insurance and savings in the stock crash in October 1929 and his and Mattie's house that you loved so there in Shaker Heights almost went too—So this is what you English profs, I think, call the 'context' for our decision then, and for our life together after that. You can see what power and influence this great figure of a millionaire could exert on us in those circumstances . . . .

"Anyway, that year, when you were one year old and completely healthy and recovered from being an 'incubator baby,' we received a grand summons to come visit Marcus and Ida in New York City, where besides having the place in Greenwich and their 'lodge' in Coronado, they kept a suite at the Waldorf-Astoria Hotel.

"We borrowed the money for train fare; it was so exciting! I was in the lower berth with you, your father in the upper. Mattie and Tom watched you as Mark and I had a leisurely dinner in the dining car. Oh, you can't imagine at that time to see the fresh red rose in its crystal vase trembling as we curved this way and that through the dark, then sudden gleams of light as we'd approach a town, then the blank black window and us cozily inside gorging on steak, asparagus, potatoes au gratin, tasting like food we'd forgotten! And I stayed awake most of the night with the shade pulled up so I could watch it 'lap the miles and lick the valleys up'— Oh, I was such a romantic girl!"

And poet, I thought, and the poet in me. But I did not reach to take her hand because I wanted her to continue.

"Their driver met us in the seven-passenger Rolls Royce and took us to the Waldorf. In their suite they had the first all-white baby grand piano I'd ever seen. Well, they took tons of pictures of us all, ordered us all around—Tom

Northway cursed and pouted and nearly took off back to
Ohio. And we would have huge breakfasts together, of
things like double thick lamb chops and Philadelphia
scrapple—aagh! And we all went to Riverside Church to
hear a sermon by Harry Emerson Fosdick, a sermon which
the General pronounced quite a bit too liberal for his blood.
And Aunt Ida made us all sit through a long and horrible
musicale and then she took me to Altmans, the only store in
New York she considered 'elegant' enough for her
patronage, and bought me five evening gowns that cost two
or three hundred dollars each and also some quite matronly
looking ensembles that I could only bring myself to wear
years later . . . . But it all, of course, was very Cinderella-ish.

"Then, the night before we were to leave, there was a
special dinner and Ida presented me with a horrible portrait
on ivory in a velvet case done from a picture of me that had
won a beauty contest when I was in college. And Uncle
Marcus, the General, dear God, Bo, he presented Mark, his
namesake, with a check for the fantastic sum of five
thousand dollars—and with a choice.

"This was the choice: They would build us a house in
Coronado, California if we would come and live by them
there, if we would leave Ohio and our parents, you
understand; or they would give us the deed to the Grand
Tarpon Inn which the General owned in Fort Myers,
Florida, contingent on our going there, if we wanted to be
on our own, and making improvements and getting the old
inn back in shape and living there as we owned and
managed it."

"I never heard this. What did you do? I think I can guess the outcome."

"Yes. Since you did not grow up in Florida or California. Very sharp of you.

"The outcome: Oh, there was a gleam in your father's eye. You can imagine. He thought about resigning his job, the one he got when you were born, but I had a word to say about that. He was the same guy in terms of getting excited about a challenge as he—is now. And he said we had to consider it at least, oh, not living by them, but the other.

"So we took off for Florida in our shiny black Auburn that he loved so. We had $5000 in the bank and a million dollar hotel in the offing, and things looked interesting until we saw what a wreck of a once fine place it was. It was all dark and dingy and worn out, the remnant of a past age, certainly not the kind of upbeat future venture that Mark Northway had in mind. Edison's home was not too far from it. That was where he and the General became such friends. That picture of them fishing together was taken on the dock of that Grand Tarpon Inn.

"So it wasn't hard for Dad at thirty and I in my young immaturity to make the right decision. It would have been a disaster, including of the spirit. And old Marcus and Ida would have bankrolled it, I'm sure, and then we would actually have been working for them, wouldn't we? No. If you ever go there, there's a condominium where the inn was. The most beautiful royal palm trees line each side of the street.

"Dad did lose his job, because of the time away. F.D.R. was inaugurated and Mark was selling glass coffee makers

185

and brassware door to door for a while, and managed to support all of us, my parents, his parents, all of us, even before he landed the job in sales out of Akron. The five thousand bucks did come in handy. The old Northways were hurt and puzzled. Well, actually Ida was furious! Because we accepted neither of their offers. The relationship was never again the same. Thank God.

"Back to your question: Would he have been better off, in his life, despite that bizarre incident I have recounted, to follow General Marcus Northway's lead?

"No. Never. In his way, the way of power and pride, the old General was kind of crazy, I'm sure a megalomaniac of sorts. Certainly a tyrant, not to mention, again, Ida! And my Mark could never have been a doctor or a lawyer! Anyway, your father was right, you know. He was always more on the side of the future than the General."

She had flushed. Her color was wonderful in that moment, eyes for the first time in years sparkling.

"Do—*you*—have regrets?"

She smiled at me, her earnest Number One. "Yes," she said. "I regret that this brandy is making me feel so detached and out of it and sleepy. Otherwise I'd have another."

The doctors in Iowa repeated the ultra-sonic treatment once more. It was unsuccessful. In the next few years my father's side became rigid, the shaking worsened, and he became bent over, weak, immobile. They never replaced the skull piece. The dent stayed in the side of his head. Then they liquidated the business and came to be with us in

Texas. My mother cared for him night and day in their new house until she had to put him in a nursing home.

He was terribly good and patient there. He would call up a smile whenever anyone even tried to make a joke. The characteristics of the disease do not necessarily include impairment of the mind. He pretty much knew what went on, though what was going on on TV or out there in the world confused him more and more. (And was confusing. Having a president assassinated in our city was confusing.) He came to hate the noise of television and to like wood fires. Even when he would come out on the weekend to visit us in July he liked a fire in the fireplace as he sat in a robe under air-conditioning. He was fully aware that my first book was published the year after his operation, although he did not try to read it. We drove him by the downtown bookstore where dozens of the brightly-jacketed books were stacked in the display window. It pleased him to see them there, well merchandised.

Since the novel was about my growing up and first college year and was set in Ohio I went back there on a trip to promote it. I stood by a stack of the books in a department store in the city where I grew up hoping to autograph it for the hordes of people who would come to greet me, then after an hour or so praying that at least one person would come by. Then I looked and saw someone. It was Baldy. He smiled, coming towards me. He already had the book in hand. I felt like that youth again, I felt like embracing him, but stood smiling back at him as I shook his callused hand.

"I bought and read it right off," Baldy said, "soon as I seen it had come out. That is some book, all right, Bo. I enjoyed reading it, this book of yours. Young Wolf, he always did say that you would make it as a writer."

"I—"

"I recognized it, Bo, that you put us in it, me and Vince."

I nodded at him, having the feeling that the crosscut saw was between us once again.

"Oh," Baldy said, smiling. "I thought you were awful kind to us. Vince, he passed, you know. Them days were good. I always do especially remember, of all the boys that worked with us, you two boys, you and Wolf."

We shook hands again.

"I'm so pleased you came."

"Yes, sir," he said. "I am glad I could come to your party, Bo."

At that point not three people in the world called me "Bo." He turned, a long, lean, ageless man, and walked away.

I went home and told Dad about Baldy, recalling how we had worked that summer, telling him how wise and just Baldy was, giving us back in conversation what we'd given him. Dad smiled and said he remembered him.

"Real nice guy," Dad said. "Repeated what you said. About my speed now."

"Well, I have to go get ready to teach. What was it old Jake Northway said, about what you have to know to teach the pigeons? Do you remember that?"

"I remember Jake Northway. He would sit in the hotel lobby there in that little town and smoke cigars he borrowed. I am sure he said something acute and adroit. Son, please help me walk into the bathroom."

He was in the hospital for a checkup.

"We're supposed to call a nurse to help you."

"I hate to ask her to go to the damn bathroom, Bo. I'm afraid she'll think I'm trying to put the make on her."

Out of the bathroom, we stood and looked out the window to the streets below, at the flow and vitality of all the people and cars of the dynamic city. I felt it pleased him to look at it. When the nurse did come in to give him the white goo for his X-rays in the morning, she said, "Would you like a spoon, Mr. Northway?"

"Bring a shovel and we'll bury it," he said.

Always when I would go to see him, when he was still in their house or later in the hospital or nursing home he would look up and smile, and say, "Hello, my beloved son."

As the pernicious thing progressed, and my mother was increasingly worn down physically and, for all she had done in constant love and care, on the brink of a desperate break towards mysticism or despair, we all did agree that it was best for him to have this other care and for her to leave the house and go into an apartment.

And he truly liked it in the nursing home. We all went there to see him just after he got settled, Joy and her kids, Frances and my daughter and I. It was a single room with good space. Some old men and women, one of whom kept trying to disrobe, sat tied in wheelchairs waiting for dinner down the hall. He would not go out there or get near them. He greeted us smiling, light in his eyes, freshly shaved, his

face thin and the dent in his skull, bare legs like smooth
white tubes as he sat in his robe in his chair and received us.

"This is the south wing," he said. "I get the sun here."

It was bright and cheerful. Out the window he had a
view of some trees, a dirt hill and a yellow tractor.

At the garage sale she had when she moved my mother
sold everything she could not take to the apartment, and
more. She wanted to get rid of all of it, she could not stand
it by now, what it stood for and the memories it brought.
She had dragged it from city to city. Now she sold her
sheets and towels and extra blankets for a quarter each. A
small vase with a painted flower on it that I remembered
from forever she gave to the postman. A set of china went
for two bucks. She kept furniture she needed for her dining
and living rooms and bedroom. She kept the yellow-green
lamp that Aunt Ida and Uncle Marcus brought to them from
China. Reluctantly she kept a trunk loaded with swords and
pictures and all the mementos of Uncle Marcus and stored it
in the garage of her apartment house. Feeling strange and
disoriented, I received Uncle Marcus' stud box and dozens
of gold and jade cufflinks I would never wear and his silk
handkerchiefs and my father's duplicitous Kappa Beta Phi
key and the grayblue-orangy-agaty ring he'd worn so long.

When they came to Texas Luke had packed up some of
the old tools and put them on the van, tools from Gramp
Tom's place and from our home place in Ohio and now I
found among them a rusty old blue bow saw. I picked it
up. Standing there in the garage of this house so many
miles and years from our place of growing up, I ran my
fingers over the old saw's blade. The prick of the blade

brought back a scene from the Ohio place of twenty years before.

I was just thirteen. He had tried to teach me how to prune our apple trees. I was sawing away at a branch with this blue saw, sawing with one hand and believe it or not holding on to the limb with the other. And the saw slipped, or attacked—a jagged, dancing blow. I stood and beheld the gash with disbelief. Then I walked around the house to the barn where my father and brother were painting barn windows, holding the hand now gushing blood out in front of me and said to him, trying to sound casual and grown up, "Hey. I cut myself."

And the memory came of how quick, strong and steady his hands were as he tore a strip from his flannel shirt, bound my wrist tightly with it and had me down our hill in the Chrysler to the hospital below for stitches in what seemed minutes. How calm I stayed, because of the strength and steadiness of his hands.

Dying was the final lesson. Soon he suffered a cerebral thrombosis in the nursing home. He did not rage, but he did not go easily. In the hospital the doctor said he should by all indications die during the night, but the lungs cleared and the heart pumped on. I went down early in the morning and sat with him and watched his heart beat on. I sat and watched him trying to live and talked to him.

And then he held on, never conscious, for more than a week.

It was the first day of October, still hot on the Texas prairie. I had to go to a morning meeting and then to my 9:30 sophomore Humanities class. I went in to it and began

191

the lesson. We were reading Plato. We finished discussing *Euthyphro* and went on to the great *Protagorus* dialogue in which Socrates proves against the sophist that virtue is not relative but one, and is knowledge; and I thought how like Socrates, with his power to see through to the heart of something, my father was, and yet also how like the super salesman of his time, Protagorus. And how the Greeks might have been either this or that, sophist or idealist, at least in their dialogues, but how mixed and contradictory are Americans in their beliefs and motivations.

At 10:20 I looked outside, through the white-framed windows of the classroom, and the whole train of thought of the dialogue and its conclusion and our discussion of it left me for a moment. I blotted out for a minute, looking through to pure blue sky. At 10:45 the secretary slipped in with a note that said that my father had died. I put the note in my jacket pocket and wound up the discussion and gave the students a stiff reading assignment. The bell rang at 10:50. I stood at the lectern as the students left the room. Some initials were carved into the top of it. Then I went to my car and drove to the hospital. He had died around 10:25, as my thoughts came back together and we rehearsed the final argument.

We held a memorial service, the Reverend Stony Van Epps presiding. Each of us, my mother, my sister Joy, my brother Luke and I, our families, said good-bye in our own ways, or did not. I remember feeling small as we sang the hymn and spoke Isaiah and Corinthians ("Love endures all things") and listened to Stony's final prayer.

That was years ago. By now I am approaching his age then. And along the way, as he would say, I've kept a handle on the tasks of life; but still at times I hear his voice, see him smile and his eyes light up, and wish I had my father's hands.

Northway Genealogy
From the progenitor Thomas Northway,
several branches are skipped to the relevant.

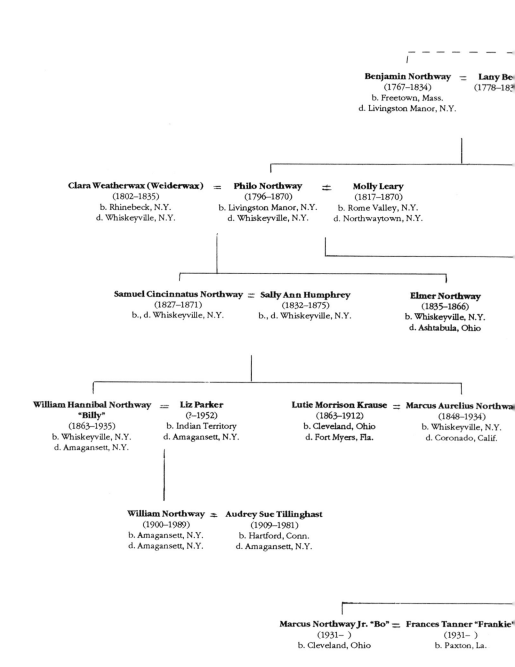

Benjamin Northway = **Lany Be**
(1767–1834) (1778–18?
b. Freetown, Mass.
d. Livingston Manor, N.Y.

Clara Weatherwax (Weiderwax) = **Philo Northway** ± **Molly Leary**
(1802–1835) (1796–1870) (1817–1870)
b. Rhinebeck, N.Y. b. Livingston Manor, N.Y. b. Rome Valley, N.Y.
d. Whiskeyville, N.Y. d. Whiskeyville, N.Y. d. Northwaytown, N.Y.

Samuel Cincinnatus Northway = **Sally Ann Humphrey** **Elmer Northway**
(1827–1871) (1832–1875) (1835–1866)
b., d. Whiskeyville, N.Y. b., d. Whiskeyville, N.Y. b. Whiskeyville, N.Y.
d. Ashtabula, Ohio

William Hannibal Northway = **Liz Parker** **Lutie Morrison Krause** = **Marcus Aurelius Northwa**
"Billy" (?–1952) (1863–1912) (1848–1934)
(1863–1935) b. Indian Territory b. Cleveland, Ohio b. Whiskeyville, N.Y.
b. Whiskeyville, N.Y. d. Amagansett, N.Y. d. Fort Myers, Fla. d. Coronado, Calif.
d. Amagansett, N.Y.

William Northway = **Audrey Sue Tillinghast**
(1900–1989) (1909–1981)
b. Amagansett, N.Y. b. Hartford, Conn.
d. Amagansett, N.Y. d. Amagansett, N.Y.

Marcus Northway Jr. "Bo" = **Frances Tanner "Frankie"**
(1931–) (1931–)
b. Cleveland, Ohio b. Paxton, La.